Santa Fe Woman

Other Books by Barbara Spencer Foster

Girl of the Manzanos
Pecos Queen
Fire in the Bosque
Fremont F. Ellis, Last of Los Cinco Pintores

Santa Fe Woman

A Novel
The Sequel to
Girl of the Manzanos

Barbara Spencer Foster

SUNSTONE
PRESS

SANTA FE

Sunstone books may be purchased for educational, business, or sales promotional use.
For information please write: Special Markets Department, Sunstone Press,
P.O. Box 2321, Santa Fe, New Mexico 87504-2321.

Book design ✦ Vicki Ahl ✦✦ Cover design ✦ Betty L. Mockel
Body typeface ✦ Centaur
Printed on acid free paper

—————————————————————————————————————

Library of Congress Cataloging-in-Publication Data

Foster, Barbara Spencer, 1927-
  Santa Fe woman : a novel / by Barbara Spencer Foster.
    p. cm.
  "Sequel to Girl of the Manzanos."
  ISBN 978-0-86534-825-7 (softcover : alk. paper)
  1. Women's rights--Fiction. 2. Santa Fe (N.M.)--Fiction. I. Title.
PS3556.O7575S26 2012
813'.54--dc23
                          2011041836

—————————————————————————————————————

WWW.SUNSTONEPRESS.COM
SUNSTONE PRESS / POST OFFICE BOX 2321 / SANTA FE, NM 87504-2321 /USA
(505) 988-4418 / ORDERS ONLY (800) 243-5644 / FAX (505) 988-1025

Lovingly dedicated to my loyal helper, Susan Barbara Foster Ames, my amazing daughter, whose outward beauty is only outshone by her inner beauty of spirit.

I

The only sound that penetrated Mardee's numb mind was the sharp clicking of her heels on the brick platform of the railroad depot. They were beating out the cadence of "Don't go, don't go, don't go. Don't leave me alone, Carter. Please don't go."

"Don't go," she muttered as he pulled her strongly into a close embrace. The coarse gabardine of his uniform muffled her words, and she buried her head in his shoulder with a shudder torn from the weakness and sickness welling up in her body. She fought to steady her trembling legs, and silently cursed her scared knees. Tortured sobs tore through her clenched teeth, and she struggled in vain to swallow them.

Carter's comforting hands gently stroked the red-gold hair that curled down Mardee's back. "It'll be fine, little sweetheart," he chanted softly. "You'll keep things going for me while I'm gone. Hell, you'll be a better lawyer than McMahon here when I get back. You'll finish your education, and between me, you, and Cabot, the McMahan Law Firm will be the biggest one in Santa Fe in a few years. I'm counting on you, girl."

Mardee felt the strong pressure of Carter's big hand lifting her face to meet his steady eyes, now clouded with love and concern for her. Blinking fast to stop the tears and regain her composure, Mardee met his gaze and attempted to smile. "I love you so much, Carter. I'll take care of things," she said in a wavering voice.

"The first thing I'll do when I get home is have a new sign made proclaiming, 'Spencer, McMahan, and Cabot.'"

Mardee drowned in the brown eyes she knew so well and attempted a wan smile. Her name on a sign on the law firm. That was a thought that rallied her bruised and faltering spirits. Her tremulous lips opened slightly as Carter bent to kiss away the tears that coursed down her cheeks. He held her slight body tightly as his lips moved on to her mouth and drank in the ecstasy of the eternal promise of her love.

The harsh insistence of the train whistle demanded their return to reality. A cloud of steam enveloped them as the train puffed to a noisy stop. Carter looked drearily at the train and then at Mardee. "I've got to head out, sweetheart," he said gently. "I'll send you a wire before I ship out in New York City." The uniformed conductor was stepping out of the train entrance holding his steel step which would make boarding the train easier for his passengers.

"All aboard," came the authoritative call of the train master.

Carter hurried toward the train, and Mardee ran along beside him on her heels. More swirls of steam engulfed the couple, and as Mardee held her hand up to her eyes and nose, she felt one last brush on her cheek as Carter clambered up the steps. "Bye, bye, sweetheart," came his words through the steam.

"Damn steam," Mardee muttered as she tried to catch a last glimpse of Carter. She saw nothing but the slim body of the train sliding down the track, belching more puffs of smoke and steam. She kept her eyes glued to the railroad track as the train faded out of sight, but finally she turned and walked across the platform with heavy steps. A couple that had just gotten off the Santa Fe Special milled around trying to collect their suitcases and children. Mardee skirted around them impatiently and turned herself in the direction of her car.

As the distraught young woman drove blindly down the rough streets of Santa Fe, turning east and then north, she only knew she had to get away from the place that had taken Carter from her so completely and finally. Alone again, she thought. So alone. Now these words chanted through her brain, and she asked herself a question she had pondered many years before. "Why?" she cried aloud. "Why do I lose everyone I love?"

The tears came again in a torrent, and the tormented girl turned the car onto a side road to avoid the traffic. After a while she realized she was on the road to the little mountain town of Pecos. The sassy Pecos River bubbled down the valley on the right side of the road. She pulled the car off the road and sat with her head on the steering wheel for some time. Finally the tears abated, and she slowly opened the door and walked down to the river. She watched the crystal clear mountain water flowing merrily to the lowlands. It doesn't have a worry in the world, she thought drearily. It just knows it will rush to join its big sister, the Rio Grande, at some point much farther south and then flow on into the Gulf Waters. I wish I knew what will happen to my life now that Carter is gone.

Mardee sat down on a rounded smooth rock by the side of the river. She and Carter had come here to this mountain valley often, she reminded herself. We courted here, she remembered, and smiled as happy memories flashed through her mind. We fished, we hiked, we picked strawberries and raspberries, and our friendship grew to adoration in all the beauty. This is the first place we'll visit when he comes home, she promised herself.

Mardee lay down on the verdant grass beside the river and let the stressful moments of the day flow away with the musical waters. She thought back over the years since she had come to Santa Fe. She had poured her heart and mind into getting an education and making a career for herself after she had experienced two devastating romantic experiences. She had come to Santa Fe mainly to be near Jeff Corbin, with whom she had secretly been in love for some time. That hadn't worked out, and he married another woman for ambition rather than love. Then she turned to the mountain boy who had loved her since schooldays, but that ended in tragedy, too, when he was shot and killed in a train robbery. When she left him in the little cemetery in the Manzano Mountains, she came back to her job in the Governor's Office, as well as to her law studies. She had met Carter McMahan, who was studying to be a lawyer, and she determined she wanted to do the same thing. A girl can study law as well as a man, she told herself.

Mardee sighed and picked a grass blade to scrape a little ant from her arm. "It's been a busy time, "she murmured. "But, now that Carter has his law degree and has opened up an office, and I am close to getting my education, this blasted war has to interfere with our plans. Damn those Germans, anyway. They've sure messed up our dreams."

Carter had received his orders to report for active duty a month ago. His commission followed, and Lieutenant McMahan was now on his way to help win this war. In the meantime, Mardee would finish school and help Carter's partner, Will Cabot, run the law firm. She had given notice at the governor's office where she had worked since coming to Santa Fe that she wouldn't be available to work there anymore. Mardee sighed and raised herself up from the grass. She would miss her political life at the capitol, but her time and energy must be spent on her own business. And, it would be scary now that Carter wouldn't be there to help her. He had become such an integral part of her life from shortly after she met him until they were married a few months ago. "I'm going to miss him so much," she wailed to the blue jay sitting across the river in a pine tree. He raucously scolded her and raised his colorful body above the limb and flew away.

Mardee stood gazing at the bird as he disappeared into the blue sky and then shook her head to bring herself back to reality. Carter is gone, but only for a while, she reasoned. I've got lots to accomplish, and I'd better get about my work. She turned resolutely and headed back to the car. "Papa would say, 'Get a move on, girl. Do something, even if it's wrong. Quit wasting time."

Mardee got in her little Ford car and headed back to Santa Fe. In a few minutes she was at the law office which was located just off the Plaza. Will looked up from his work when she walked in. His desk was strewn with files, and he obviously was very busy. He gave Mardee a swift look and then said, with relief, "I'm so glad you are here. I'm swamped, and I need you to do some research for me." Mardee grinned patiently at her husband's partner and said, "That's why I'm here, Will, to help you. Just put me to work"

Later Mardee drove up the driveway of the little stucco building she and Carter called home and let herself into the empty house. "This house almost seems big without that big moose of a Carter here," she laughingly told herself. She glanced quickly at the mantel of the pretty rock fireplace and fixed her eyes on the wedding picture that set in its place of honor. Carter's shock of dark hair fell rebelliously over his forehead as his laughing eyes proclaimed his happiness on this special day. He loomed over Mardee, but she held her small body straight and proud. Her luxuriant copper hair was pinned into captivity under a lace mantilla. Her small waist was emphasized by the tight bodice draping the curves of her youthful body. Her large eyes were filled with pride and wonder as she proclaimed to the world her love for this man and her hope for the future. Mardee stood for a moment staring at the picture and found herself mouthing these words incredulously, "You didn't have a clue that day, girl. Not a clue. But I've learned a lot since then." Then Mardee smiled in spite of herself. She knew she could face the months ahead, no matter what happened. "I can do it," she said with resolve as she waved at the picture.

Just then there were two short knocks on the door through which she had just entered. She turned to answer the knocks, but the door opened, and her father stood framed against the blue of the sky. "Papa," she screamed. "You are really here!"

Ben Spencer looked his daughter up and down slowly, and then opened his arms. "Hello, Mardeebird," he said in a husky voice, calling her his pet name. "It's good to see you."

"And you, too," Mardee said breathlessly. "Oh, Papa, you always come when I need you." Ben's gaze turned quizzical. "What do you mean?"

"Carter left today, Papa. He's off to the war. He'll be shipped to Europe in a few days."

"I'm sorry, daughter," Ben said. "But a lot of them are going now. You know, your brother has been gone for three months. He's in the middle of the action."

Mardee held her father more tightly. "You and Mother Spencer must be so worried about Floyd. Have you heard from him?"

"One brief note. He was there and all right at the time. There have been some big battles since, though."

For the first time Mardee focused on a girl who had moved to her father's side. Her dark disheveled hair almost hid half of her face. Her hands nervously clutched a small worn bag. Her eyes were eloquent with anxiety and an unspoken plea.

"Who?" Mardee asked.

The girl answered her question. "I'm Lola. Don't you remember me?" There was hurt and frustration in her big brown eyes.

"Of course, Lola Tompkins. Now I see it is you. I'm just surprised since I didn't know either one of you two were coming."

Ben Spencer cleared his throat. "Mardee, you wrote that your new house has two bedrooms. Lola needs a place to stay for a while, so I thought maybe you could take her in."

"Of course," Mardee said hesitantly. "But, she's been working for Mother Spencer since I left, so why is she not staying with you?" The puzzled expression on her face expressed her confusion.

"Show Lola where her room is," Ben said brusquely. "While she unpacks, I'll tell you why she is here."

Mardee took Lola to her small guest room and helped her put her clothes in the dresser, the one piece of furniture in the room besides a bed. When she returned to her father, he said before she asked him, "Lola is in the family way. She needs a place to stay for a while where people don't know her. I thought maybe you could help her."

"Of course, Papa," Mardee said uncertainly. "I'm working and going to school, but I'm sure I can get Mrs. Roberts or Mrs. Sanchez to help us."

"Well, we just had to get her out of there. It will be better here where no one knows her." Ben spoke hurriedly but a little haltingly. This was an embarrassing subject for him. "She has about four months to go. She'll be fine by herself when you are working, and when her time comes, you must get someone to help. I'll leave some money for you."

Mardee's heart was suddenly touched by her father's demeanor. He looks old to me, for the first time, she realized. This is hard on him. "Of course, I'll take care of her," she hastened to assure her father. "You can leave the money for the doctor bill when the baby comes."

"If I was here, I could deliver it myself," Ben said with a note of pride in his voice. "But I doubt you could do that."

"You are so right," Mardee said wryly. "We'll get a doctor."

Lola came back into the room at that moment, and Mardee noticed her thickening waist now showed plainly without her loose coat covering her body. She looks so young to be having a baby, Mardee thought. Impulsively, she ran to the girl and embraced her with her strong arms. "You can stay with me, Lola. It will be like old times. You can help me, and I can help you. My husband left today, and I'll be so happy to have someone here so I won't be alone. Welcome to Santa Fe, dear Lola."

Lola turned her soft brown eyes gratefully up to Mardee's sparkling turquoise ones. "Thank you so much, beautiful Mardee. You have always treated me like a sister. I thought you would help me. Gracias, mi hermana."

2

Mardee felt herself coming out of the hazy tunnel of sleep, but she didn't open her eyes. She lay there in the comforting warmth of her bed, instinctively resisting the reality of the day. Slowly she moved her hand to the other pillow. She felt no tousled head with strong familiar features lying next to her. Suddenly she opened her eyes, sat up, and hit the pillow viciously with one motion. "Oh, Carter," she wailed as she flung herself down on the pillow. "What am I going to do? What will I do without you?" Soft knocks on her bedroom door interrupted her agony. "Yes?" she said faintly.

Her door opened slowly, and Lola entered the room. "Good morning," she said uncertainly as she took in the tear stained face turned away from her. "I have made breakfast. Won't you come and eat?"

Mardee wiped her wet face with the end of the sheet and sat up in bed. She held out her arms to the other girl and said in a broken voice, "Lola, it is so good to have you here with me. Thank you for coming."

"Thank you for having me," Lola said quietly.

The girls held to each other for long minutes, and there was no need for words as each felt the comfort of the other's love. Lola finally pushed away and took control of the situation. "Wash your face and come and try the pancakes," she said firmly. "You must work today, yes?"

"Yes," Mardee sighed. "Will needs me at the law office, I'm sure. No time for tears, right?" She suddenly remembered her father. "Where's Papa," she asked.

"He's already eaten and is on his way to the Gross Kelly Office. He has some business with that company. He said to let you sleep in a little while. That's different for your father to let anyone sleep extra time in the morning, isn't it?" Lola shook her head in wonder.

Mardee smiled and put her feet over the edge of the bed. "That's right," she agreed. "But, I'd better get up before he comes back and finds me still in bed."

Lola left Mardee to her morning ministries. When she emerged from her bedroom, her transition was complete. She wore a smart blue suit which swirled softly around her slim ankles. The tight jacket with a wide red belt emphasized her small waist. A bright red scarf tied at her throat gave her appearance the spark her personality demanded. She walked across the room with quick steps, her classic blue pumps emphasizing her confidence. "How do I look?" she demanded as she pivoted on her toes, while her long auburn hair formed a bright halo around her face.

"Oh Mardee," Lola gasped. "You are so beautiful. You look like an angel."

"Not quite," Mardee contradicted with a short laugh. "I am a Gibson Girl. I'm part of a new breed of women who work at a career and demand respect for our accomplishments. I'm almost a lawyer, Lola, and I'll be helping in my husband's firm while he's away. I'm not an angel by any stretch of the imagination."

"All right," Lola agreed. "But you are a mighty pretty Gibson Girl, whatever that is."

"You and Mother Spencer haven't heard of Gibson Girls on the ranch in Eastview?" Mardee asked in an amused voice as she sat down at the table.

"Well, no," Lola commented seriously. "You know what we do on the ranch."

"Work," Mardee said dryly. "Just work. I remember." She buttered her pancakes and poured syrup on them. "But we had fun, too," she added.

"Oh, yes," Lola agreed. "Do you remember the dances?"

"Oh, yes," Mardee sighed. She took her first bite of breakfast and chewed thoughtfully. "These pancakes are wonderful, Lola."

"I will cook for you every good thing," Lola said quietly, "and I will clean your house. I will help you all I can for letting me stay here."

"Of course, I'll let you stay here. You are a part of home, and I've missed home so much. We will help each other, we two girls from the Manzanos." Mardee spoke in a tender voice of the mountains where she had lived and smiled warmly as she continued to eat her breakfast. "It's too bad Carter isn't here to eat these pancakes. I'm afraid I haven't taken the time to do much cooking for him lately. I was so busy with school and working part time at the office. But, now I won't be taking any classes this summer, so I'll have extra time. I'm only lacking two courses for graduation, and I'll finish them up in the fall. That's when I'll really be busy again. That's when you will really be a help to me."

Lola smiled as she refilled Mardee's juice glass. Then a shadow came over her face. "But that's when the baby will come, too."

"That's all right," Mardee hastily assured her. "We'll both be very busy. But, we can do it."

"Oh, yes," Lola agreed as her face softened at the thought of her baby.

Mardee contemplated her food and thought of their conversation the night before. She had hesitantly asked the question, "Who is the father?" Her own father had looked away, and Lola's face had become a frozen blank. They hadn't answered her question. In her mind, she figured the age Lola must be now. I'm twenty-two, she thought. Lola must be eighteen or nineteen. Poor girl.

Lola seemed to have read her thoughts. She said slowly, "Some day I will tell you about my baby. But, I thank you so much for giving me hope. Now I can have my niño where people won't know me and shame me and the baby. You are an important person here in Santa Fe. People like you, and they will also like me and my little one. Thank you, from the bottom of my heart."

Mardee impulsively jumped up from her chair and ran to Lola. "No one will dare criticize you or the baby. I promise you. I'll do everything I can for you and this child."

A raucous honk permeated the emotional atmosphere of the kitchen, and Mardee realized her father was back. She patted Lola and went quickly to her front door and out to the truck parked in front. "Mornin', Dad," she said cheerily. "Did you get your business done?"

"Yes," he retorted just as cheerily. "I have signed a contract with the Gross Kelly Company to provide them with two loads of lumber a month. Santa Fe is starting to grow, and they need building materials. I'll go back through Albuquerque and buy a truck to haul lumber. So, I'll be seeing you often this summer, my pretty one." Ben smiled fondly at his daughter and touched the end of her nose lightly.

"Wonderful," Mardee said in a delighted voice. "Maybe you will be here when the baby comes."

"Don't count on that," Ben said with a shake of his head. "Babies never cooperate with anyone. You can handle it, daughter. Get a good doctor lined up to deliver it and watch over her while she carries it. She's a healthy girl, so everything should be fine."

I hope," Mardee said in a shaky voice.

Ben's face turned serious. "You've got a hard row to hoe for the next few months, Mardee, with Carter gone and your job and your school, and Lola here, too. But I raised you to know how to face adversity. As I said, you can handle it." Mardee looked into her father's determined face, and suddenly she felt his strength infiltrate her uneasiness. "I'll do my best, Papa," she said firmly.

"I know you will, and now I have to head south. I'll see you soon. Make sure Lola drinks lots of milk and gets her exercise. Don't let her lay around in bed. She's got to be strong for her delivery."

"Yes, Doctor Spencer," Mardee said merrily. She felt her usual optimism returning. She waved as Ben Spencer drove off in a cloud of dust. Then she experienced her usual hurtful parting pang as she watched his car take him out of her life again, but she knew her confidence was stronger. Her father always had that effect on her.

Mardee went back in the house and told Lola she could weed the flower beds after she finished the household chores. "That way you and the baby will get some sunshine," she said with a grin. Then she added, "You know, this baby is already a very important part of our lives." Lola smiled as she patted her bulging middle.

Mardee hummed one of the old songs her father used to sing and drove the few blocks from her house to the office. She walked up the flight of stairs to the law office with firm footsteps. She greeted Will and went into Carter's office and set her briefcase down on his desk. She sat down in his thick leather chair and leaned back as she viewed the neat desk with a picture of the two of them smiling back at her. "You'd better not distract me," she warned as she glared at the happy couple in mock irritation. Then she smiled and picked up the picture and gave it a kiss. As she grinned at it, Will came into the room. He walked with his usual hesitant steps, and said nervously, "I've got to go to the courthouse, so I'll leave you to hold down the fort here. I need to do some research on some mining claims for this case I'm working on, and I may not be back until three or four o'clock. If you need me you can call me at the recorder's office. All right?" "

"Of course," she assured him. "Take all the time you want. I have a lot of typing to do."

As Will shuffled off, Mardee called after him, "Thanks so much for all you do, Will. I appreciate you so much." Will turned his head briefly, and Mardee caught his red embarrassed expression. Poor Will, she thought. He's so conscientious he hurts, but we are so lucky to have him while Carter is gone.

Mardee turned to gather the papers she would be typing, but her eyes lingered on the picture again. She remembered the day it was taken—such a happy day. She and Carter had returned from their honeymoon trip to Mexico City. When they arrived at the home they had purchased, a group of friends were waiting for them with a variety of luscious food and music.

The party started, and everyone ate and danced and made merry until the wee hours of the morning. It was daylight when the revelers finally left, and she and Carter lay down on their new bed to spend what was left of their first night together in their own home. She closed her eyes and relived the passion of the beginning of their lives together. She felt the shivers of love's unrequited desire course through her body as she thought of the long days and nights ahead of her without Carter. She looked at the faces in the picture as they strained toward each other with unapologetic longing. Life will be so empty without you, dear Carter, she cried inside herself. How long, will it be? My own heart will surely die.

With a long sigh, Mardee turned her eyes from the picture and put paper in her typewriter. She started to type, but footsteps in the outer office permeated her consciousness. She jumped up from her chair just as a figure appeared in her door. "May I help you?" she said automatically. The figure advanced toward her with quick steps, and before she actually computed her visitor's name, strong arms enveloped her. "Mardee Spencer, how are you?" came delighted words in her ear.

"I'm fine," Mardee replied breathlessly as she clung to the encircling arms. Her entire being now knew who held her, although her eyes were closed. "Oh, Jeff! Jeff, how good to see you!"

Almost as quickly as Mardee had fallen into her visitor's arms, she realized she should not be there. With an effort, she pushed slowly back and gazed up into the face that had been such an important part of her past life. She looked alternately at the thick blonde hair waving back from the high brow, the classical nose, the beautifully sculptured lips, the strong square jaw, and the blue eyes desperately searching her face. "I didn't know you were in town," she said in a husky voice. "I can't believe you are really here." The small finger on her right hand slowly reached up and traced his high cheek bone wonderingly, but she instantly snatched the hand away and put it behind her back.

Taking a step backwards in obvious confusion, Mardee met his eyes and said, "Excuse me for greeting you so dramatically. This is a strange day for me. I'm missing my husband who has been called into active duty in the Army, and he left for overseas just yesterday. Also, my father departed this morning to go back to Eastview, so I'm missing him, too. Seeing you is quite a surprise."

"I didn't mean to unnerve you," the surprise visitor said apologetically, but the look of pleasure on his face belied any misgivings he had. Then his eyes clouded as he said, "You mentioned your husband?"

"Yes," Mardee said, and her voice sounded too loud and defensive. "I was married last November to Carter McMahan. He's a lawyer from Las Cruces, and this is his law firm. I'll be working with his partner, Will Cabot. I almost have my law degree, too." Suddenly Mardee felt pangs of her old resentment toward Jeff Corbin coming back, and she withdrew a step and lifted her chin in a stance of cool guarded defiance.

"Congratulations!" Jeff said warmly. "I have thought of you often and hoped you would do just this. You will make a wonderful lawyer."

"Thank you," Mardee said in a barely audible voice. "Why are you here?" she asked more clearly.

"I'm looking for a house to buy," Jeff replied. "My job in Washington, DC has been culminated, and I am coming back home. I have missed Santa Fe dreadfully. I want to see all my old friends again, and I want to live and work in this fabulous city."

Mardee found herself at a loss for words, and all she could say was, "Oh?"

Jeff looked at the uncomfortable girl and decided he should not infringe on her time any longer. "I know you're busy," he said easily, "but I just heard from the manager of the building I'll be renting that your office is here, and I couldn't resist coming upstairs to say hello. I have some other appointments to keep, so I'll be on my way. I plan to be here about a week to make preparations for coming back. Would it be possible for us to meet for lunch tomorrow and get caught up on our lives? I'd like to see you before I leave."

Mardee nervously caught her breath. The resentment was gone now, and she found herself wanting to say a definite yes to Jeff's proposal, but caution overrode her impulse. "I probably won't be going out for lunch tomorrow," she said hastily. "Perhaps you could stop by another day and see how my workload is."

"It doesn't have to be tomorrow," Jeff said easily, "but I do want to see you before I leave. Please tell me that will be possible."

"I guess so," Mardee said weakly.

Before she could change her affirmation, Jeff turned quickly and started for the door. "See you soon," he said lightly. He raised his hand in a slight wave. Then he was gone.

Mardee walked back into her office like a robot and sat down slowly on her chair. "Jeff Corbin!" She said in a wondering voice. "Jeff Corbin" She felt as if her heart would pound through her chest. "Dear God, what am I going to do?"

3

Mardee tried to be interested in the tasty supper Lola had waiting for her when she got home, but a few bites of the hot soup and delicious roll were all she could manage. Lola looked at her anxiously and asked, "Don't you feel well?"

"I'm a little tired," Mardee replied. "It was a hard day at the office."

"I suppose you don't want any rice pudding, either?"

"No, thanks. I think I'll take a walk."

"Oh, could I go with you? I'd like to see the neighborhood."

Mardee looked into the hopeful face of Lola and couldn't refuse her request. She's been here all day, and she's ready to get out of the house, she thought.

"Sure," she said listlessly. "Take off your apron and we'll get some fresh air."

Mardee was lost in her own thoughts as the girls headed for The Plaza. Lola remarked enthusiastically about the homes and shops they passed. Her eyes were big when Mardee pointed out the impressive Presbyterian Church. "And that's the new library," Mardee continued. "You must go there and check out books to read. They have a good assortment."

The thought of going in that large building and being able to choose books to take home to read made Lola's eyes sparkle even brighter. "This is a dream town," she said dramatically.

"That's what I thought when I came here, too," Mardee said with a slight smile. "It is a little different from Eastview, isn't it?"

"Oh, yes," Lola said ecstatically.

"But don't ever forget there is no place like home," Mardee admonished seriously.

The girls walked on in silence until they found a bench in The Plaza and sat down under the shade of a big tree. "We'll sit here a while and watch the people go by," Mardee said as she retreated into her own thoughts again. I can't believe I reacted that way to Jeff, she repeated to herself for the hundredth time. Here I am, grieving over Carter being gone, and Jeff appears and I greet him like a long lost lover. I had put Jeff totally out of my life. I didn't even like him anymore. I certainly love my husband. I miss him, and I want him back, and I am miserable without him. Why was I so happy to see Jeff? What kind of a woman am I?

Mardee put her head in her hands as she berated herself for her actions. She rocked back and forth and sighed deeply. Lola watched her friend with compassionate eyes and finally put her hand softly on her arm. "Mardee, do you want to talk? Do you want to tell me what is bothering you?"

Mardee shook her head. The girls sat in silence for several minutes. Mardee finally lifted her head and said, "I saw Jeff today." Lola remained silent but gently pressed Mardee's hands which were clenched tightly in her lap. Mardee turned to Lola abruptly and said through clenched lips, "Lola, I was so happy to see him. I let him put his arms around me. I put my arms around him. What's wrong with me, Lola? Do you think I'm a bad person?"

Lola spoke slowly and thoughtfully, "Maybe you're upset because you were happy to see an old friend. No, Mardee, I don't think you are a bad person. I think you are a lonely person."

"I love my husband, Lola," Mardee said vehemently. "I love my husband who is fighting for his country."

"Of course, you do," Lola said just as vehemently. "You are not a bad person, Mardee."

"All right, thanks," Mardee said as she rose from the bench. "Let's go home. I've told you part of the story about Jeff, but I'll tell you the rest of it as we walk. Then maybe you'll understand why I am doubting myself."

The golden New Mexico sun was starting to disappear behind the mountains to the west. The adobe buildings they passed took on the hue of the setting sun. "No wonder the early Spanish explorers thought they saw a city of gold when they explored the New Mexico Territory. The city is almost a golden city this time of day."

"I love it," Lola said. "And we are golden girls in this golden city."

Mardee put her arm around Lola and murmured, "I'm so glad you're here, little Eastview girl. But, let me tell you about the famous Jeff Corbin."

Mardee grew silent again. Finally she said, "I fell in love with Jeff Corbin when I came to Santa Fe five years ago He gave me my first kiss, and I had hoped he'd be the only man I'd ever kiss. I was young and naïve, and I thought he loved me as I loved him. I expected him to marry me, but instead he married someone else, a girl whose father could help him with his political ambitions. He has been working in Washington, DC, and now he's coming back to Santa Fe. When I saw him today unexpectedly, I fell into his arms like a lovesick goose. And Carter has been gone only one day. What's wrong with me? I don't think I can trust myself anymore."

Lola stopped and faced Mardee with authority. The shorter girl put her finger up near Mardee's face and said firmly, "You listen to me, Mardee Spencer McMahon. You are upset because your husband is gone. Jeff was a friend to you before he became your sweetheart. You were happy to see an old friend today. You would have given him a hug if Carter had been here, but since he isn't, you feel guilty. You love your husband, it's that simple. Don't make something out of nothing. You're too smart for that, Mardee."

Mardee stood stiffly silent for a long minute as she looked wonderingly into her friend's face. Finally she said, "How did you get so smart, Lola? You were just a sweet little girl when I left the ranch."

Lola's smooth face changed subtly, and the hurt in her eyes was obvious before she dropped them and said, "Much has happened since you left. I hope I have learned a few things. I'm not a little girl anymore."

Mardee felt her old confidence coming back. "No, we are both young women, and this is an exciting time for women, Lola. I must go to a meeting tomorrow night where I'll be the speaker. You could come with me if you'd like."

"What will you be speaking about? Lola asked in awe.

"About women's suffrage" Mardee said loudly and clearly.

"What is that?" Lola asked, her face mirroring confusion.

"That's the right of a woman to vote," Mardee said jubilantly. "Women have been treated as second class citizens long enough. We've never been able to vote because, I suppose, the men don't think we're smart enough to do that. Women all over the country have gotten organized and are demanding that a constitutional amendment be added, giving us this very important right. I'm the leader for this movement in northern New Mexico, so I attend many meetings and talk to women about demanding their rights. We have quite a large group that is fighting for this amendment here, and all over the United States."

Lola's eyes were wide with wonder. "How exciting," she said. "Of course I will help you." Remembering how Lola's father had abused his wife and children, Mardee knew immediately why she was interested.

The excited young women were back at the house now. Mardee opened the door and said, "Let's go in and eat some rice pudding. Suddenly, my appetite is back, and you need to give that baby some healthful rice pudding. Don't ever forget it, Lola. Women are smart enough to vote as well as being beautiful, talented and good mothers and wives. We are really quite amazing!" Two lighthearted women walked briskly into the kitchen.

4

Mardee parked her car in front of the big white house on Grant Street. She sat for a moment just to enjoy the view of the house. She had stayed here after she came to Santa Fe to work five years ago. Judge and Addie Roberts had invited her to stay with them until she got used to the big city. Santa Fe seemed like a huge metropolis to her after having been raised in the little mountain community of Eastview. She loved the beautiful home and its hospitable owners. They had made her stay pleasant and had always been there for her anytime she had problems. They had become a second mother and father to the naïve rural girl. "I couldn't have made it without you two," she whispered to herself.

Judge Roberts had passed away suddenly this past winter. Mardee had kept in close touch with Addie since her tragedy, spending time with her every weekend. But Addie was adjusting well to her new situation. She continued to take in renters and boarders, as well as teach piano lessons. What an amazing lady, Mardee thought as she swung the steel gate open and walked into the well kept yard. She looked at the grass under the huge elm tree where she had read and dreamed her girlish dreams. There were many hours spent there imagining my future with Jeff, she remembered. "What a waste of time," she said aloud with a grimace.

Mardee opened the door and was greeted by Addie who was down on her knees scrubbing the hall. "Don't scrub another spot," she ordered. "I'll finish this for you."

"You won't have to talk me into that proposition," Addie sighed as she got up off her knees and sat down in the nearest chair. "I don't have much left to do, but I would appreciate your help."

26

Mardee set to work with the scrub brush while Addie fanned her face and relaxed. "Lord- o'- mercy," she finally said as she got back on her feet, "I'm gonna fix us a sandwich and a cup o' tea. It's nigh on to lunch time."

"Don't fix much," Mardee instructed. "I had a big breakfast."

After finishing cleaning the hall, Mardee came in the kitchen where Addie had laid out sandwiches, tea, and cookies for their lunch. "That there sandwich has meat from a beef roast I cooked yesterday," Addie explained. "I made several sandwiches, and the boarders can eat them when they come in. Lunches are pretty informal around here on Saturdays."

"I always love your food," Mardee said with gusto. "Everything you make is so good."

"You said you had a big breakfast. You must be doin' a little more cookin' than usual."

"No," Mardee laughed. "I have someone with me now, and she cooked my breakfast this morning."

"Who?" Addie asked. She knew Carter had left a few days ago.

"Lola Tompkins from Eastview. She was a neighbor girl. She has been living with the family for several years. She came to help Mother Spencer when I left. She's a sweet girl, and bright, too. She just didn't have much chance with her family. Her father was an Anglo, and her mother was a Spanish girl who died in childbirth. He marries women who aren't very good to his children. I'll tell you about old Lou someday. Anyway, he wanted Lola to stay with Mother Spencer and learn to cook like she does. Also, I think he wanted to be sure she was safe. His current wife was abusive to her."

"Oh," Addie said, looking intently into Mardee's eyes. "But, why is she here now?"

"My father brought her a few days ago and asked me to let her stay here a while. Addie, she's pregnant, and Papa wanted her away from Eastview. I don't know the details of the pregnancy. I just know I have to help Lola at this time."

Addie nodded her head in understanding. "I see. Of course, you must help her."

"Well, I'm going to need your help," Mardee said seriously. "I don't know anything about babies, before they are born or after they come. I need to get Lola to a doctor. Who should I take her to see?"

"Doctor Amble," Addie said without hesitation "He's down on Lincoln Street. He's very good."

"That's where I'll take her." Mardee's countenance brightened, and she said, "Do you remember when you and the judge delivered the Gonzales baby? That was an exciting time for me. I'd never been involved in anything like that before."

"I remember," Addie said. "I remember delivering many babies with the judge. But that was all in the past. I let the doctors do that now."

"I'll get off work early one day next week and take her to see the doctor," Mardee said. Both women were silent as they ate their food. Mardee suddenly laid down the remainder of her sandwich and continued, "Addie, I'm worried about Lola. She's young, and this is her first child. I hope there are no complications."

"She's young and strong, so the chances are there will be no problems. Don't worry, my dear,"

Mardee looked into the plain but happy face of her friend. "You've done so well since you lost the judge. How do you do it, Addie?"

Addie put her work worn hand over on Mardee's smooth one. "I don't really do it, Mardee. I depend on my Lord Jesus to help me. I can't do it by myself. But with His help, I can get through. Read the twenty-eighth chapter of Matthew, Mardee. This chapter tells of the events after Jesus came out of the tomb and went back to see his disciples. They didn't want him to leave them and go back to his Father in Heaven, and He said as He left, 'Lo, I am with you always.' The important word there, Mardee, is 'always.' My husband is gone, true, but my Lord is with me always, so I don't have to worry. Understand?"

Mardee turned wondering eyes on Addie. "I must read my Bible more. I must have Lola read this passage, too. I know she must be anxious about this baby." Mardee paused for a moment and added, "And I'll read it when I feel so alone."

"Read it every time you have a problem. It works," Addie said softly.

Mardee smiled and said, "By the way, are you ready for the Suffrage Meeting tonight? I'm hoping we have a good crowd."

"I'm ready," Addie pronounced in a firm voice. "You can have the parlor. I'm inviting all my roomers to attend, also. Of course, most of them are men."

"That's all right," Mardee said with a giggle. "We'll convert them, too."

Mardee rose. "I must go, Addie. I've got a little work to do on my speech, and I must make petition forms for people to sign to send to the Congress. We must stress the importance of getting equal rights for women to vote. The more names we have on our petitions, the more attention the congressmen will pay to us."

"You are so right, Mardee, and I know you're doing a good job on this project here in northern New Mexico," Addie said. She embraced the leader of the Suffrage Movement, and Mardee left the house on Grant Street with renewed determination to fight the good fight for this worthwhile cause.

Mardee spent most of the afternoon in her office practicing her speech and typing forms. When she went home, she told Lola to forget about supper and get ready and go with her to the meeting. "I want you to hear what we are discussing," she told her. "And, perhaps you can be of help to me. If there are any Spanish ladies there who don't understand English, you can be my interpreter." Mardee spoke Spanish, but knew Lola was proficient in the language, having had both Spanish and Indian stepmothers.

Lola was excited at the thought of going to an important meeting, but she worried about her clothes. "I'm getting too big for most of my clothes," she said. "What will I wear?"

"Just wear any dress, and put a loose shirt over it. That should camouflage the little fellow. By the way, I told Mrs. Roberts about the baby today. You don't have to worry about help with the baby."

The young women dressed for the meeting; Mardee in a flowing pale green shirtwaist dress, and Lola in a brown skirt with a loose white over blouse. They drove happily to the house on Grant Street.

Addie Roberts greeted people at the door and directed them to the meeting room. She had set about fifteen chairs in a circle around the room. When it appeared everyone had come who would be there, Mardee rose to welcome the group and address them.

"Frances McDonald, our ex-governor's wife, had planned to be here, but as you all know, her husband recently passed away, and she feels it's a little early to go out quite yet. But, I would ask you to send her a card, or drop by and see her and express your sympathy. She was a wonderful first lady, and I know she would appreciate the thoughtfulness. Some of you are aware of the fact that I worked for Governor McDonald, and it was my privilege to become well acquainted with both the governor and his wife. They are fine people. Frances has given her support to the Women's Suffrage Movement since its inception. She would have loved to be here tonight to speak and meet all of you."

Mardee proceeded on with her speech. "The fight for women's suffrage goes back to 1848 when the first Women's Rights Convention was held in Seneca Falls, New York. Four years later Susan B. Anthony joined in the fight, stating that 'the right women need above every other is the right of suffrage.'

"It took forty-one years of proposing the Constitutional Amendment, 'The right of citizens to vote shall not be abridged by the United States or by any State on account of sex,' before the Territory of Wyoming became the first part of the United States to allow women to vote. The other western states of Utah, Colorado, and Idaho joined Wyoming in allowing this right to women. In 1912, Theodore Roosevelt's Progressive Party became the first national political party to have a plank supporting women's right to vote. The tide was beginning to turn for us.

"Now we must put enough pressure on our congressmen so they will pass this amendment. I'm hoping I can persuade each one of you to sign a petition in favor of Women's Suffrage. I will see that these petitions get to our congressman."

Mardee then opened the meeting for questions. After a discussion period of about thirty minutes, the meeting was adjourned, and while the guests ate cookies and drank punch, they also signed the petition. Mardee had Lola explain to two Spanish women the gist of what she was promoting, and the women happily signed their names on the petition.

Mardee had just whispered to Addie how pleased she was with the success of their meeting when a lone gentleman walked into the room. Mardee looked up to face the smile of Jeff Corbin.

"I didn't tell you that Jeff is one of my boarders," Addie said hastily.

"Mrs. Roberts announced at supper about your meeting," Jeff said easily. "I thought I would join you."

"Of course," Mardee said in a much calmer voice than the chaotic emotions she felt inside should have allowed her. "We will be happy to discuss with you any points we have brought up."

"Could I have the floor for a few minutes?" Jeff asked courteously.

"Of course," Mardee said again. "Ladies, we are honored to have with us tonight, Mr. Jeff Corbin, who is a former member of Governor McDonald's cabinet and more recently a legal advisor in the Attorney General's Office in Washington, DC. Mr. Corbin wants to say a few words to us. Proceed, Mr. Corbin."

Mardee sat down and looked up at Jeff. Her mouth was smiling, but her eyes were challenging. "Be careful what you say," was their warning.

Jeff smiled at his audience and started out in a soft hypnotizing voice. Mardee was reminded of the speech he had given at the Statehood Celebration in Eastview. He had seduced everyone with his beautiful words and voice. Certainly her, but she knew she must not dwell on that day and those feelings.

"I've known Mardee Spencer McMahan for many years," he was saying. "I met her at a Statehood Meeting which she attended with her father. Ben Spencer was an active voice for statehood in his part of the state. Mardee started interpreting for him at these meetings when she was a very young girl. I was amazed at her maturity and ability for one so young." Jeff paused, and then continued. "Yes, and I was also captivated by her beauty."

Mardee felt the hot flush in her cheeks, and there were discreet smiles from the crowd. Jeff went on.

"When Governor McDonald became the first statehood governor, I went to work in his administration. Mardee's father expressed his desire for her to work there also. I knew Mardee could do the job, so I recommended her to the governor. He interviewed her and immediately gave her a position in his office. She did her work exceptionally well, and when I left the administration to take a job in Washington, DC, Mardee was advanced to a position of greater responsibility in the governor's office.

"Now, it doesn't make much sense that a girl with so much ability could work in the governor's office, but she could not vote for that governor, does it? Well, that's exactly the situation in which Mardee found herself.

"I have been gone and lost track of Mardee, but it does not surprise me to find her leading the parade for Women's Suffrage. I approve of what she is doing, and I remain very proud of her, as always. She will also become a New Mexico lawyer soon. A woman named Myra Bradwell led that fight for women to be accepted to the state bar. Now Mardee Spencer carries on the banner for equal rights for women. Excuse me, I meant to say Mardee Spencer McMahan. She got married on me while I was gone." There were more smiles and a few twitters.

Jeff concluded his oration by saying, "I urge you all to join in this fight and help Mardee all you can." He smiled and turned away to enthusiastic clapping.

After Mardee had concluded her meeting, she joined Jeff and thanked him for his good words. He graciously accepted her thanks and said, "I feel sure the Congress will pass this bill by early next year. It will take about a year for the states to ratify it. So, all your work will not be in vain, my dear."

"I'm glad to hear that," Mardee said in a purposely calculated impersonal voice. "May I get you something to drink?"

"No, thank you," Jeff said pleasantly. "I'm on my way to another meeting. Thank you for letting me add my two cents worth."

Jeff walked away, and Mardee took a deep breath before she continued socializing with everyone. People didn't linger too long, and Lola helped Addie straighten up her kitchen while Mardee sent the guests on their way. But she managed to arrange another meeting place at the home of one of the interested guests before everyone departed. Another meeting at another home with other guests; that was her goal these days, along with a few marches. Most important, more meetings and more signatures for Women's Suffrage.

When Mardee and Lola got back home after the meeting, they both relaxed and ate a bowl of soup Lola had cooked earlier. When Mardee finished, she pushed back her bowl and stretched her arms above her head. "That was good, but suddenly I'm very tired."

"I can see why," Lola said with a smile. "That was quite the meeting, and Mr. Corbin certainly added to it, yes?" Lola's dark eyes danced with mischief as she studied the face of her friend.

"You are a little devil," Mardee said as she lifted her chin and stood straight and stiff. "I had all those women signed up before he made his speech. It was really unnecessary."

"Maybe," Lola replied. "But, he's quite a speaker. I was impressed."

Mardee gave Lola a sharp impatient look and turned to go to her bedroom.

At that moment there was a knock on the door. Mardee turned to see who was at the door this time of night. She quickly drew the door open. A messenger stood there with a telegram held in his hand. "Mrs. McMahan?" he asked.

"Yes," she said shortly, reaching for the piece of paper.

Mardee forgot the boy at the door and ripped the envelope open. She hastily perused the message and lifted large unbelieving eyes to Lola. "It's from Carter," she gasped. "He leaves on a troop ship tomorrow for Europe. Oh, Lola, he will soon be on the front lines."

Lola shut the door in the messenger's face and ran to embrace Mardee. All thoughts were of Carter now. The eloquent speaker at their meeting was totally forgotten. The war had wiped all considerations of anything or anyone besides Carter from their minds.

5

Mardee opened her eyes and looked blankly at the lacey pattern the morning sun made as it was reflected through the curtains and onto the ceiling. "Carter is on a ship heading across the ocean," she whispered. "I hope he gets there safely." But even if he gets there, he will soon be fighting in a trench, she thought as terror caught at her breath. When will I ever get him back?

Mardee had been watching the papers closely since Carter left. It seemed that the Allies were starting to win more battles, but there were still many casualties. Maybe this conflict won't last too much longer after he gets in the thick of the fray. Mardee turned over impatiently and put her arms around Carter's pillow. Her thoughts went back to the first time she had met him. It was on a train going home for the Christmas vacation, she remembered. A handsome young man had sat down beside her, and she had practically ignored him. He told her he attended the University of New Mexico in Albuquerque, but her thoughts were all on home and Frankie, so he made little impression on her. Then he had come by the ranch on his way back to school. She was still grieving over Frankie's death then, and she still remained unimpressed with Carter McMahan. He had asked if he could come to Santa Fe and visit her, and she had discouraged him, so she didn't see him for several months.

Carter finally came to Santa Fe many months later and appeared at Mardee's office. Enough time had elapsed, so Mardee's hurt was starting to subside. They went out to lunch, and Mardee found herself actually enjoying being with a young man again. Carter impressed her as a serious person, but one who liked to have fun. She decided he was a man of strength and principles, and certainly he was very handsome in an unsophisticated way. She surprised herself when she realized she was laughing again and looking forward to his visits. However, the memory of Frankie persisted, and she maintained a definite distance between herself and her admirer. This went on for many months, but Carter religiously came to see her every weekend and was content to be just her friend.

When Carter received his law degree, he came to Santa Fe to set up an office. Mardee was surprised to find herself relieved he wasn't going some place else to work. She realized she had grown so used to his presence she would miss him if he completely left the area, and as her respect for him grew stronger, their friendship deepened and finally matured into love. The day came when Mardee let her barriers down between them, and the passion she thought had died within her as a result of Jeff's unreturned love and Frankie's lost love burst forth in an unquenchable flame hotter and brighter than it had ever been before. Finally Mardee returned his kisses with a fire that matched his own, and on the banks of the Pecos River, the promise to love each other forever was made and consecrated.

Mardee and Carter were engaged for a full year before they married. Carter was working hard to establish a law business. Finally the clients started coming, and Carter talked his college friend into joining the firm with him. Will Cabot was a bright conscientious lawyer in whom Carter had complete confidence. With Mardee joining the firm when she finished law school, life was an exciting promise, and the young couple looked ahead with confidence to their future.

Mardee and Carter had been married in the home of Addie and Judge Roberts. Her father and stepmother and her youngest brother, Roy, had come for the wedding. Governor McDonald and his wife, Frances, were there. Several government workers attended, since Mardee had worked at the capitol for five years. Some of the teachers from Mardee's school, the Loretta Academy, were there, as well as her good friend from school,

Raquel Sanchez Riley, with her husband, Stewart, and little girl, Angela. As Mardee repeated the solemn wedding vows after Judge Roberts, she never looked away from Carter's steady brown eyes, and she meant every word of her promises. I vowed to love him forever, she thought, but then a slight prickling of conscience intruded on the young wife's thoughts. Then, why were you so glad to see Jeff? She interrogated herself with troubled dismay.

"I do love my husband," she burst out angrily. "I'm just lonely, and I was glad to see a friend."

Lola opened her door at that moment. "Talking to yourself?" she asked curiously.

"Oh, just mumbling a little," Mardee said as she swung her feet to the floor.

"Breakfast is served," Lola said brightly. "Put your robe on and come out to the kitchen."

The girls sat down to eat, and Lola looked at Mardee with a different expression in her eyes. "What is it?" Mardee asked anxiously. "Do you feel all right?"

"Wonderful," Lola said. "Do you want to feel my baby kick? He's really active this morning."

Mardee jumped up and ran around the table. Lola took her hand and guided it down to her distended stomach. She carefully placed it and held it lightly in the middle of her belly as she looked at her with an expectant smile. "Do you feel him kick?"

Mardee felt slight movements like the fluttering of a butterfly under her fingers. "I do," she shouted. "I feel him." She lifted her hand after a few moments and went back to her breakfast.

"Do you notice we are calling the baby 'him?'" Mardee asked.

"It will be a boy," Lola said complacently. "I will call him Robbie."

"Little Robbie Blue Eyes," Mardee said, but as her eyes met Lola's brown eyes, she added, "or Little Robbie Brown Eyes."

"His eyes will be blue," Lola said quietly.

"Then his father is an Anglo?" Mardee asked without thinking.

Lola didn't answer, but she got up quickly and started clearing the table.

"I'll go get dressed for church," Mardee said as she tried to keep her voice natural. "Do you want to go with me?"

"Yes," Lola said, "but could we go to the Catholic Church?"

Mardee thought a moment and said, "Of course. I'll take you to Saint Patrick's Cathedral. It's so beautiful that you are bound to receive a blessing."

Lola smiled happily as she went about her chores. She was baptized Catholic by her mother, Mardee thought, so it's natural for her to want to go there. I'll take her today and show her where it is. I'll enjoy being inside the church myself. The Presbyterians can do without me for once."

The young women went to church in their best Sunday dresses, and both looked lovely. Mardee wore a pale blue summer skirt and crisp white blouse, and Lola wore a short summer jacket over her sleeveless voile dress. "Can you tell?" she asked Mardee.

"Not yet," Mardee said with certainty.

"It won't be long," Lola said.

Mardee enjoyed the service in the elegant church, and her jumbled thoughts of the morning settled down. She prayed for Carter and felt confident God heard her.

After the service as Mardee and Lola started to walk down the steps of the church, a jovial voice stopped them in their descent. "Mardee, Mardita! Stop for the minute. Un momento, por favor."

Mardee turned to see Miguel and Teresa Sanchez hurrying down the steps after her, so she stopped and waited for them. "Como esta, mi hita?" Miguel asked warmly as he took Mardee's hand. "You are muy bonita today. How are you, mi querida?"

"Hello Miguel, my friend," Mardee said gleefully. "How are you?"

"Bien," and Miguel's eyes went to Mardee's companion. "Quien es?" he asked with a big smile.

"My friend, Lola Tompkins, from Eastview," Mardee said. "She has come to stay with me for a while."

"Con mucho gusto," Miguel said. "I am so happy." Miguel could speak English, but he often reverted back into his native Spanish.

"You must come home with us for dinner," Teresa said as she interrupted the conversation.

"Yes, yes. You will come?" Miguel asked delightedly. "I take you and bring you back."

"That would be lovely," Mardee retorted, "but we will drive. I have a car now, you know."

Miguel shook his shoulders expressively. "Okay. Es bueno."

Raquel and her family walked up just then, and she and Mardee fell in each other's arms. A tall red-haired man followed carrying a toddler. Mardee transferred her excitement to the child and said, "Raquel, she is so beautiful. Hello, little doll. Hello, pretty Angela. Come to your Aunt Mardee."

Angela came into Mardee's arms with no hesitation. Lola noted that the child's hair had the same bright red gold color as Mardee's. Then she noticed the bright red hair of the father. That explains it, she thought.

Mardee apologized to Stewart, Raquel's husband, for unintentionally ignoring him and introduced everybody. When the excited chattering started abating, Miguel said, "Vamanos. I'm hungry. Let's go."

As Mardee and Lola drove over the mountain road to the Sanchez Ranch, Mardee told Lola about her friend, Raquel "I met her at the Loretta Academy," she explained. "We clicked from the first day. We sang in the choir and acted together in a play at school. I often spent the weekends with Raquel at the ranch. The Sanchez Ranch is an old Spanish Land Grant, so these people have lived in New Mexico for a long time. Their original ancestors came from Spain. They are genteel people who stand on the highest principles. I would trust Miguel and Teresa with my life. Raquel is like a sister to me. I know you will like her."

Lola looked away toward the distant mountains and remarked, "I wish I had grown up with a family like that."

Mardee shook her head sadly. She remembered the abuse the Tomkins children had endured, but she knew old Lou Tomkins had loved Lola in his own way. "Your daddy loved you, Lola. He was so proud of you. He thought you were so smart."

Lola looked at Mardee with sad eyes. "Do you really think so?"

"I'm sure of it," Mardee drove the car over a steep little hill and pointed at the ranch buildings that lay below. "That's the Sanchez Ranch. Isn't it beautiful?"

"It makes me lonesome for the Spencer Ranch," Lola said with a remote look in her eyes.

"That's why you'll feel better after you visit here," Mardee said emphatically.

Teresa took a pork pot roast smothered with onions, carrots, and potatoes out of the oven. There were fresh tortillas, apricot jelly, spicy pickled beets, and green chili to complement the vegetables and roast. Custard pudding seasoned with cinnamon made in the traditional Spanish way was the dessert. Both Mardee and Lola ate until their stomachs felt uncomfortably filled.

"You're the best cook in New Mexico, Teresa," Mardee said as she rose to help clear off the table.

Teresa blushed and said with a wave of her hand, "Es nada, mi hita. You can do it. Raquel does."

Raquel shook her head and said, "I'd rather ride with Papa and Stewart."

Mardee washed the dishes, and Lola dried while Raquel put things away and kept an eye on her little one.

Amid their girlish chatter, Raquel suddenly asked, "When is your baby due, Lola?"

Lola looked surprised and glanced hastily at Mardee. "Tell her," Mardee responded as she mouthed the words.

"I'm not sure," Lola said hesitantly.

"We are going to the doctor this next week and get a definite date,"

Mardee said. "Lola thinks she is due about the end of September."

"You have not put on much weight," Raquel said kindly. "You still have a good figure. You should have seen me. I was as big as a house from three months on."

"Oh dear," Lola said nervously.

"Don't worry about it," Mardee said lightly. "You'll do fine."

"If you need help when the baby comes, let me know," Raquel volunteered. "Mardee will be working, and I would be happy to come in and take care of you and the baby."

"Thank you so much," Lola said as she looked from Mardee to Raquel. Impulsively, she added, "I will tell you about my baby's father some time."

Teresa had listened quietly to the conversation. "We'll be happy to help you in any way, Lola. Just let us know." She walked over to Lola and gave her a warm hug.

Mardee finished wiping off the table and counter and changed the subject. "Raquel and Teresa, I have a petition for you both to sign. You know, I'll be sending these names into Washington, DC to be read by our Congressmen."

"These are the petitions asking that women be given the right to vote?" Raquel asked.

"Yes," Mardee responded. "I want you both to vote in the next election."

"And you want to run for election some day, yes?" Raquel said coyly.

"Could be," Mardee said with a toss of her long golden curls. She dug the petition out of her purse and handed it to Raquel. "Would your father sign, too, and your husband?"

"Si, senorita," Miguel said with a grin. "I sign." Stewart ignored the question.

Raquel walked out to the car with Mardee. Lola had remained behind to talk with Teresa. Mardee put her head close to Raquel's ear and said, "I saw Jeff a few days ago. He's here looking for a house. He and his wife are moving back to Santa Fe."

Raquel's big brown eyes opened even wider, and she asked, "Did he look you up?"

"Yes, he totally surprised me. I had no idea he was back in town."

"How did you feel when you saw him?" Raquel asked quietly.

"I collapsed in his arms, if you can believe it. After the way he treated me. And my husband had just left to go overseas and fight for his country. I am so ashamed, Raquel. He wants me to have lunch with him before he goes back to Washington, DC. I'm not going to do it. Why does he have such an effect on me, Raquel?"

"Well, he was your first love," Raquel said sagely.

Stewart had come up behind the girls unnoticed while they were talking. "What's that about first love?" he asked playfully.

Raquel looked up at her tall husband and said easily, "I was telling Mardee how strong first love is. You were my first love, querido." Raquel smiled radiantly up at her husband, and his questions were buried in burning desire for his beautiful Spanish wife.

Raquel nestled into Stewart's strong arms and said, "My first love and my only love. You know, Mardee, when Stewart was gone with General Pershing fighting the Mexicans, I thought I would die. I'm so glad he's home to stay this time. His service is over."

"Yes," Stewart said happily. "I'll never leave this señorita again, and Miguel has another hand to help with the ranch."

"Don't remind me of men away from home fighting for their country," Mardee protested. "I don't know how I'll survive with Carter being gone."

"You're a strong woman," Stewart said. "You'll make it. One thing I know for sure is that he has a very good commanding officer. General Pershing takes care of his men."

"Small comfort," Mardee said under her breath.

"Let me know when your next suffrage march is," Raquel said as Mardee started her engine, "and Angela and I will go with you."

"It's a deal," Mardee said with a smile, ignoring Stewart's scowl. "We might as well start this child out right!"

Lola waved to the Sanchez clan as long as she could see them. "I'm so glad you brought me here today," she said. "I feel I have friends already."

"Of course you do, Lolita," Mardee said as she blew her a kiss. "And we're all going to take care of our girl and her niño."

"I know," Lolo said with a satisfied smile.

6

Mardee buried herself in her work as the summer progressed. She and Will spent long hours in the office to keep up with their workload. "We're doing it, Will," she encouraged one evening when they locked the door to leave after twelve hours of work. "We'll have things in good order when Carter comes home." Will nodded his head and smiled. I'm so lucky to have him, Mardee thought.

Mardee picked up a newspaper as she passed the La Fonda Hotel. That was the last thing she did every day as she headed for home. After supper she read every line of the paper and tried to get a feeling for how the war was going. She had gotten two short notes from Carter. They gave little information, but she got the impression he was in France. He had mentioned a French Poodle in one letter. The word in front of Poodle was censored out, but Mardee was sure the blacked out word was French. He didn't even like that kind of dog, so she surmised he was trying to tell her his location. And from her reading in the newspapers, she knew there were Allied offensive operations going on northeast of Paris. She felt sure he was in the thick of the action.

Mardee allowed herself to worry only at night after she went to bed. She was really too busy to let her anxiety intrude during the day. She actually had more thoughts about Lola than Carter most of the time. The doctor had set the baby's arrival date somewhere around the middle of September. It was now the end of June. Time was going fast, and Mardee caught her breath at the thought of the actual delivery. She was afraid she wouldn't be much help when the time came.

A car was parked in front of her house when she drove into her driveway. She went in the front door and saw a woman sitting on the parlor settee. She was a young attractive Spanish lady and looked vaguely familiar to Mardee. The woman rose and extended her hand graciously. "I hope you don't mind," she said apologetically. "I need to talk with you, and your friend asked me to sit and wait because you would soon be home from your day's work. I am Rosa Hidalgo. I met you at one of your Suffrage Meetings."

Mardee took the woman's hand and smiled warmly. Now she remembered the woman. "Hello, Rosa. I do remember you. It was at a meeting in Las Vegas, yes?"

"Yes," Rosa retorted excitedly. "You told me you would like to take part in our Old Town Fiesta in July. I'm here to invite you to do just that."

"Wonderful," Mardee said, beaming at her guest.

"You may set up a booth in the park to pass out your brochures and have people sign your petitions. And if you would like to be part of the program, that would be fine. You mentioned you might want to sing or dance. Of course, we'll have a great deal of Spanish dancing. If you remember, I'm a dance teacher in Las Vegas, and my students will be performing."

"I probably would be able to work something up," Mardee said slowly. "I'll make a speech, of course, but perhaps a little something extra would intrigue people and get them more in the mood to sign their names."

"I will arrange it," Rosa said with finality. "Plan on the evening of the fifteenth of July, about eight o'clock. That should be a good time for you as there will be a big crowd then. My dancers will start performing at seven o'clock when it is cooler, and you can give them a rest in about twenty minutes. They'll need it by then. Their fast flamenco dances take a great deal of energy. Well, all the Spanish dances do."

Lola was standing quietly in the door of the kitchen. Mardee turned to her and said, "Lola, you can help me. You're a great singer, and you could sing some Spanish songs. Maybe I'll do a little dancing to some of your songs."

Lola gave Mardee an agitated look, and she disappeared into the kitchen. Rosa nodded her head and said, "Whatever you do will be fine. Plan on entertaining one way or another for about twenty minutes while my dancers rest. And now I must be on my way back to Vegas. I'll be counting on you. I wanted to do something to help you with your suffrage project, and I think this would be a good time for you to be there."

Rosa was out the door in a flurry of Spanish skirts, and Mardee stood for a moment digesting what had just happened. "Now I'm an entertainer," she said with wonder. "Lola, you'll have to help me," she said more loudly as she headed for the kitchen.

Lola stood in front of the stove looking overwhelmed. She put out her arms and said, "Look at me? How can I perform looking like this?"

Mardee's eyes dropped to Lola's middle. The pregnancy was very noticeable now. Mardee was silent a moment and then spoke persuasively, "I'll figure out something. Don't worry about it, Lola. I'll think about this and come up with something." She gave Lola a quick hug and added, "I'm starved. First feed me, and then I can think."

After the supper dishes were washed and put away, Mardee and Lola sat on comfortable chairs in their enclosed patio and exchanged ideas about their coming performance in Las Vegas. "I know," Mardee said as she snapped her fingers in excitement. "You could sing, *Cielito Lindo*, first in Spanish, and then in English, and I could create dance movements to go with the music. For example, when you sing, 'In Mexico 'neath the mountains' glow, to the plain below, comes the maiden,' I could dance gracefully down from the back of the stage. And when you sing, 'What a prize with her tender size, and her laughing eyes, romance laden,' I could dance some romantic movements and twirl around the stage alluringly to dramatize what you're saying. You could be singing in the background, sitting down behind a tree, and could hardly be seen. That would work, wouldn't it?"

"I guess so," Lola agreed reluctantly. "But when did you learn to dance?"

"I've always known how to dance," Mardee said gleefully. "Don't you remember how I danced in Eastview?"

"Well, yes, but that was dancing with a partner."

"Well, I don't have a partner now. I can dance by myself. Actually, I have taken some ballet classes at the college when I had some extra time. The teacher said I was good, and I should pursue it, but I don't have time. But I think I learned enough to create a dance while you sing."

"Are you sure you can camouflage me?" Lola asked doubtfully.

"Oh yes, my love. All they will see is your beautiful face and hair. And they will hear the haunting excellence of your voice. I've heard you singing here in the kitchen. You have a lovely voice, Lola."

"Thank you, Mardee." Excitement was beginning to build in Lola, too. "I've always loved to sing, but I've had no lessons like you with your dancing."

"You're a natural," Mardee assured her. "You don't need anyone teaching you to sing. You were born knowing." Mardee tweaked a lock of Lola's long dark hair and retired to the living room to read the paper. "I've got to check on the war," she explained.

Later Mardee called to Lola who was still in the kitchen, "The American Marines have captured Belleau Wood. I'm sure that's in France. They are taking back the German's ill-gotten gains."

Lola heard what Mardee said, but she didn't comment. Her thoughts were totally on this exciting development that she would soon be singing for a large audience. Her dream of a lifetime was going to come true! "Thank you, God," she whispered. "Gracias, mi Dios."

7

Every evening was practice for Mardee and Lola who were getting ready for their part of the performance at the Las Vegas Fiesta. Mardee's speech was the easy part for her. She would say essentially the same thing she had been speaking about for months. Women in America were capable of voting and should have that right. They wouldn't stop fighting until they were recognized as first class citizens in this country. And she completely believed in what she was saying, so the words came easily and effectively.

However, Lola was nervous about singing. The thought of facing a large crowd of strangers was disconcerting to the mountain girl.. "I'm afraid I'm being very presumptuous to think anyone wants to listen to me," she confided in Mardee.

"Everyone wants to listen to the girls from the Manzanos," Mardee laughingly assured her as she danced gracefully around the living room. "Don't worry, mi hita. I promise you will be the star of the night. You truly have a very special quality in your voice."

"Sure," Lola said with a sad face. "I will make them want to run or throw up."

"Just don't you throw up," Mardee admonished with a smile.

Lola's stomach still wasn't entirely free of nausea. Lola brought her hands to her face in the attitude of prayer. "Holy Mother of God," she prayed softly.

"Come on," Mardee directed impatiently. "Let's do our song again. You start singing, and I'll make my debut from the back of the stage. Be sure to open your mouth and let that pretty voice out. We want people to hear what you are saying. Remember, you are a beautiful maiden coming down from the mountains to win the hearts of all the young men in the valley."

Lola took a deep breath and did as she was directed. She closed her eyes and concentrated on the words of the song. She knew the song well; they had sung it in school when Sadie Spencer was the teacher at Eastview. Her voice rang out, vibrant and true, and she sang the teasing lyrics with a flirty undertone. At the end of the song, Lola bowed her head coquettishly, and Mardee pirouetted prettily on her toes in a whirl of skirts.

"I think we have it," Mardee said breathlessly. "Your song is perfect. Hopefully, I can remember my routine. I think I change it every time I do it."

"That's because you feel it," Lola said shyly. "You are sharing with your audience the passion and love you feel inside."

Mardee glanced sharply at Lola. "You amaze me, you little wildwood flower. How do you know so much?"

"I just feel it," Lola replied with a shake of her shoulders.

"And that's what makes your singing so beautiful, too," Mardee commented. "Go on to bed while I eat. I don't want you to get too tired, you know. Dream of being a star!"

After lunch the next day, the performers headed for Las Vegas. "I hope it isn't too hot today," Lola observed.

"We're going farther north, you know," Mardee said. "It will be cooler there."

As they went over the mountains to their destination, Mardee concentrated on her driving. The road was rough with uneven ruts left from a recent rain storm. Lola drank in the beautiful scenery. The pine trees and quaking aspen trees reminded her of home. But she opened her eyes with a start when she found herself worrying about the treatment of the younger children left at home. To take her mind off this picture, she said, "Tell me about Las Vegas. I've never been there."

Mardee liked history, and she had enjoyed going to this old Spanish town when her law duties took her there. "Las Vegas is really two towns in one," she said. Gallinas Creek runs through the middle of the town. Old Town is on the west bank of the creek, and East Las Vegas is on the other side. It became a stage stop for travelers going over the Santa Fe Trail. That was back in about 1833."

"Soon it will be one hundred years old," Lola said as she figured the numbers in her head.

"Right," Mardee concurred.

"Which part of town are we going to?" Lola asked.

"Old Town, where the park is. There is also a beautiful old hotel there called The Plaza."

Mardee turned north and drove slowly toward the hub of the town. She watched for celebrating drivers as well as excited children scooting mindlessly across the streets. Within a few minutes she was circling the park looking for a parking place.

Rosa Hidalgo waved exuberantly to Mardee from the park. "Let me help you," she called as Mardee parked and picked up her box of brochures and petitions.

Rosa led the young women to a booth set up under a huge cottonwood tree. "You'll be in the shade here," Rosa explained. "You shouldn't get too hot. But you'll be where everyone can see you so you can tell about the Women's Suffrage. People here don't know much about that. But after they see you perform, they will be interested in you, and they will listen to you."

"I hope you're right, Rosa," Mardee said with a smile. "Thanks for all your help. I think the first thing Lola and I will do is have a cold drink at The Plaza. I want to show her that lovely old hotel."

The girls walked across the street from the park and went up the steps to the entrance of the hotel. As Mardee pushed the heavy door open, she looked at Lola, and the mountain girl's eyes mirrored the excitement she felt. "Fiesta time in old Las Vegas," she said as she put her arm around Lola's thick middle. "Don't you have that baby today, at least not before you sing."

Lola gave Mardee a reproachful look and stared at the beautiful furnishings of the lobby. Comfortable couches and big soft chairs conveyed a warm welcome to the hot travelers. Lola wanted to succumb to the invitation, but Mardee pushed her on into the spacious dining room. "Let's have some lemonade and a cookie," she suggested. "That will revive us."

The lunch rush was over, and there was only one other couple in the restaurant. Mardee led the way to an oak table in the far corner. "We can hide and relax here," she explained.

A waitress in a stiffly starched brown and yellow uniform brought the treats to the table, and the girls settled down to relax and enjoy their food and surroundings. Mardee knew this was probably the fanciest dining room Lola had ever seen, and she enjoyed the look of awe that illuminated her face.

"I can't believe I'm really here," Lola whispered between long sips of her cold beverage. "I have never seen anything so gorgeous."

"I spoke here once at a dinner," Mardee said. "I knew you would like it. Now, aren't you glad you came?"

Before Lola could answer, a tall figure loomed over their table. Mardee raised her eyes to a handsome blonde gentleman, and it took her a moment to realize the man was Jeff Corbin. He was smiling and bowing and saying in a warm voice, "Mardee, what a pleasant surprise."

Mardee scrambled to her feet, knowing she must look like an awkward country bumpkin. "Hello Jeff," she managed to greet him. "I never thought of seeing you here." Then she remembered her manners and introduced Lola.

Jeff bowed slightly over Lola's hand and kissed it and murmured, "Charmed, I'm sure."

Lola looked flabbergasted and stood as if in a trance as she stared at the unexpected visitor. Then she visibly gained control of herself and said, "Charmed, also. I'm so happy to meet the famous Jeff Corbin."

"Oh, I'm not famous," Jeff protested. "More people know Mardee in

Santa Fe than Jeff Corbin. Anyway, may I present my daughter, Elizabeth. Beth, say hello to the pretty ladies."

Jeff pulled a small girl from behind him as he spoke. Her hair was neatly done in long blonde ashen ringlets caught with a pink ribbon that matched her three tiered ruffled skirt. Long dark lashes curled over her cornflower blue eyes. "Hello," she said shyly as she held out a small hand to Mardee.

Mardee was almost in stunned shock before this little beauty. Jeff's daughter, indeed! But she recovered enough to take the proffered hand and say, "Hello, Beth. You are so pretty. I love your ring. Where did you get that?" She pointed to a ring with a pink stone worn on the third finger of her left hand.

The little girl withdrew her hand and looked up at her tall father and said with absolute love and faith shining from her flawless face, "My daddy."

"How nice," Mardee said unsurely. She was wondering what to say next, but another visitor suddenly joined their group.

A tall blonde woman with a perfect coiffure stood by Jeff's side. "Oh, I've found you, darling," she said in a hurried voice. "Father wants me to join him at his board meeting which starts shortly. Could you keep Elizabeth with you for a couple of hours?"

"No problem," Jeff said quietly. "Dear, I would like you to meet an old friend, Mardee Spencer McMahan. This is my wife, Heather Corbin."

Something in the woman's superior attitude brought Mardee back to reality, and she regained her poise and said, "Please meet my good friend, Lola Tomkins."

The woman briefly acknowledged Mardee and Lola, and for a moment her light blue eyes met the warmer colored eyes of Mardee with an icy cold and almost challenging expression. Then she took her daughter's chin in her hand and gave her distinct instructions. "You will stay with Daddy, my pet, until Mother is finished with the meeting. You be a good girl. Do you understand? Mother will be back to you soon."

Beth nodded her head in a mechanical way to her mother. "Yes ma'am," she said.

"Join us for a cold drink," Mardee invited.

"I want an ice cream cone," Beth entreated. "Please."

"Your mother wouldn't like you to soil your pretty dress, love," Jeff said softly.

"Please," the child repeated.

"All right," Jeff said. "After all, you're a big girl now. We'll ask the waitress for a napkin to protect your dress from any spills."

Lola made a quick decision. "If you will excuse me, I will take my lemonade into the lobby and sit on one of those comfortable couches. Maybe I can even lie down and rest a while. I am suddenly tired."

Lola was gone before Mardee could protest, and before she hardly knew what had happened, Jeff and Beth were seated with her.

Jeff ordered a dish of ice cream for Beth and a cup of coffee for himself. While the delighted child carefully spooned ice cream into her rosebud mouth, Jeff turned his attention to Mardee. "I can't believe I ran into you," he repeated. "Heather's father is here on Santa Fe Railroad business. He's on their board. They chose Las Vegas for the site of their annual meeting, so she wanted to see him while he is this close. Her folks live in Kansas City."

"That's nice," Mardee said coolly.

"I'm sorry about Heather," Jeff said. "She's excited today about being able to see her father and sit in on one of his meetings."

"Your daughter is lovely," Mardee said, pointedly ignoring the reference to Heather. She felt the woman had treated her condescendingly and rudely.

"What are you doing here?" Jeff asked curiously.

"Lola and I will be part of the program this evening," Mardee replied. "We'll do a song and dance number, and then I'll give my suffrage spiel. Better stick around and watch us," Mardee said with a smile. The negative residue of Heather's short appearance was fading. She suddenly felt in control of her situation, and she wasn't going to worry about Heather. Furthermore, she was enjoying visiting with Jeff and his daughter. She was drawn to Beth immediately.

"How old is she?" she asked with interest.

"She's four years old, right, Bethy?"

Beth held up four fingers.

"You are so lucky to have her," Mardee said sincerely. "She's as smart as she is pretty."

"No children for you?" Jeff asked.

"No," Mardee said firmly. "We want no children until Carter is home to stay. Until then, I'll work at my job and finish my degree this fall."

Jeff looked off in the distance when Carter's name was mentioned. Mardee impulsively asked, "Jeff, are you happy?"

Jeff shrugged his shoulders. "As happy as anyone, I guess. How about you?"

"Very unhappy now that Carter is gone," Mardee answered.

"How long have you been married?" Carter asked as he looked intently into her eyes.

"I told you we were married last Thanksgiving," Mardee answered. "We were married by Judge Roberts." She smiled at Jeff, and she knew both were thinking about the night Jeff had brought her back to the house late after the Santa Fe Fiesta. She remembered that both of them were very unnerved at the thought of facing the judge, but he had been nice and understanding.

Jeff smiled and looked off into the distance. "That seems so long ago," he mused.

"Only five years," Mardee said. "But a lot has happened in that length of time."

It's unbelievable what has happened," Jeff agreed. "And it's sad to come back to Santa Fe and find the judge gone. The flu?" he asked.

Mardee shook her head affirmatively. "It got many people in this state. My family was fine. They said they didn't go any place all winter long so they wouldn't catch the bug, but one of the neighbors lost so many family members they just piled them up on the porch until spring came, and they could bury them. The snow was so deep, and the ground so frozen that burials had to wait." Mardee shuddered as she thought of this gory scenario.

"I know," Jeff said. "It was bad in the northeast, too."

Jeff and Mardee quit talking and their gazes locked together. Jeff suddenly reached across the table and covered Mardee's right hand which lay on the table. "I've missed you, Mardee. I've missed you so much."

For a moment Mardee met Jeff's eyes and drowned in the depths of them. She felt like the same love-struck girl who had loved this man when she first met him when she was fourteen years old. But she shook aside these feelings and said with determination, "We've been friends a long time, Jeff. It's natural to miss each other."

"Yes, I guess so," Jeff muttered. He hastily added, "But now I know I can see you occasionally and talk with you, can't I? Just as a friend?"

Mardee hesitated a moment and said with a bit of her usual vitality, "Of course, Jeff. Just as friends." She emphasized the word, friends.

"Thank you," Jeff said as he gave her hand a gentle squeeze and turned it loose. "And I do wish I could hear you speak tonight. But I heard you speak when I was here before. You do a good job."

"Oh, thank you, Jeff. You are so kind. But tonight I'm going to dance, too. Lola will sing, and I will dance."

"Perhaps I'll still be here, and if so, I'll manage to hear you," Jeff said with a smile.

"I would love that," Mardee said as his eyes held hers steadfastly.

Beth had finished her ice cream and had sat quietly while the adults talked. Now she broke into the conversation. "Daddy, I'm finished with my ice cream. Can we go now?" Then she looked apologetically at Mardee and said, "You can come to see us some time in our new house."

"Mardee focused her eyes on the little girl and said, "And where is your new house?"

"Up the hill," Beth said with a vague gesture.

"We live on Canyon Road in Santa Fe," Jeff said.

"Oh?" Mardee said. "Up with the big bucks people?"

Jeff shrugged his shoulders. That's where Heather wanted to be. Her father wanted us there, also."

"Goodbye," Beth said as she took her father's hand.

"Mardee laughed and said, "There's no doubt she's ready to go. Goodbye, sweetheart."

Mardee watched the proud father and the precocious little girl walk away and felt a momentary pang of emptiness. "He's so lucky," she said in a low voice. "Well, I'm happy for him, and someday I'll have my children."

Just then Lola appeared at the dining room door. "Jeff paid for our drinks," she said."What a handsome devil he is." she added Then she changed her teasing expression to a serious one and said, "Don't you think we should be getting over to our booth? We should be talking to people about Women's Suffrage, you know."

Mardee jumped up and collected her scarf and purse. "You are right, my dear." She said briskly. "On with the show. We're goin' to knock 'em dead, you know." She knew her thoughts of Jeff and his darling little daughter must be put aside.

8

The afternoon sun was low on the western horizon as Mardee followed Lola up the steps to start their performance. Lola sat on a chair at the rear of the stage and pulled a black mantilla around her body. Mardee posed in the forefront looking radiantly over the crowd as the flaming sun to the back of her brought out the fire in her hair. When the first vibrant notes proceeded from Lola's throat, Mardee swung her lithe young body around and lifted her arms passionately toward a distant unseen master. And as Lola captured the emotion of every note she sang, Mardee depicted the lyrics dramatically while she swayed and moved to the story the song articulated. She wooed the audience with all the emotions of the spectrum, from joyfulness to sadness and from flirtatiousness to submissiveness, and finally to charismatic exultation. When she took her bow at the end of the song, the wild cheers broke in unison. Shouts of, "Bravo! Bravo!" split the air, and when Mardee motioned for Lola to join her, the noise intensified. They bowed and waved to the crowd and started to make their way off the stage. It was impossible to speak because of the noise, so the two stars went back to their booth and sat down flushed and breathless. Mardee squeezed Lola's hand and said jubilantly, "You did it, and it was beautiful. I am so proud of you!"

"You were fantastic, Mardee. It was easy to sing to that wonderful dancing."

"Maybe people will be more interested in my booth now," Mardee said with a giggle.

And the crowd did indeed start gravitating toward the suffrage displays. Mardee stood up and greeted everyone with a dazzling smile. She gave an inspired talk, interspersing it often with the Spanish translation of her words to clarify her meaning. Her audience listened to her as if hypnotized, and the awe in the many faces pressed toward her was unmistakably inspired reverence for her and her cause. When she invited people to come forward to sign petitions, long lines formed and many names were signed without any hesitation.

As the first rush of signatures was finished, the crowd thinned and drifted to other areas of the park. Mardee sat down and took a hankie from her low-necked blouse and wiped the perspiration from her brow. "I'm sweating," she whispered to Lola, "and I'm sure real stars never do that."

"Few of them probably work as hard as you do," Lola said.

Mardee replaced her handkerchief and glanced up to see a lone young man standing at their booth. His hat was pulled down perkily over one eye, and he was smiling suggestively as he looked directly at her neckline. "Good place to hide your treasures," he remarked as dark expressive eyes met her startled green eyes.

Mardee recovered her poise and asked quickly, "Did you wish to sign a petition?"

"Not really," the young man said smoothly. "I don't truly believe in equal rights for women. The only rights they should have are the ones we give them after they take care of us."

Mardee felt the blood rush to her face, and anger replaced her confusion. "You are not in the right place, sir," she said icily.

"Oh, but I am," the smooth voice continued. "I'm sorry for my remark. I really don't feel that way. I guess I was trying to get a rise out of you. And you do look so pretty when you are angry. I'll sign your petition." The man chuckled and smiled broadly as he wrote his name. Then he looked up and continued. "Let me introduce myself. I am Jetson Spangler, and I'm associated with the Santa Fe Drama Company. I saw your performance, and was very impressed. I am interested in you two ladies. Where do you live, and would you consider a performing job?"

Mardee and Lola stared at each other and then back at this astounding stranger. "We live in Santa Fe," Mardee said hesitantly. "I have a job in my husband's law firm." She looked at Lola and pointed a finger in her direction. "She might be interested in your offer." She nodded encouragement at Lola's shocked countenance.

The stranger turned his gaze to Lola, and said questioningly, "Well?"

"I...I...I...," Lola stuttered. "Not now, I think."

Mardee hastened to explain, "Lola is hesitating because of her condition. However, her baby will be here in a short time. She does have a lovely voice, and she is a beautiful girl. You would, of course, pay her for her talent? And, what did you say your name was, sir?"

"Call me Jet. And are you sure you couldn't manage some evening work? We're going to start try-outs for a new play entitled, *The Yanks are Coming*. We'll be using the music of George Cohan, songs like *Over There*, *Grand Old Flag*, *I'm a Yankee Doodle Dandy*, and *So Long Mary*. I can visualize your singing and dancing in some of these songs, especially the *Mary* song. I'd like for you to audition. And yes, we pay a salary to all our performers. Your friend could sing in the chorus even though she is with child. You're not pregnant, are you?"

"No!" Mardee said with undisguised aggravation. "My husband is in France fighting in the war right now."

"I'm sorry," Jet said, and his voice sounded sincere. "It might be a good thing for you to do," he continued. "Being very busy will take your mind off your anxieties."

"I don't know what to say, Jet," Mardee said honestly. "You have taken us by surprise, I can assure you." Mardee sat down weakly on her chair and looked helplessly at Lola.

Lola suddenly stood up and said with determination, "I think I might interested in this job. Would you tell me more about it?"

Jet rummaged in his shirt pocket for a moment and handed Lola a card. "Our theater is located out on the Old Pecos Trail Road. I could visit with you any afternoon. You could ask the girl in front to take you to my office. I'm the director." As Jet turned to go, he smiled and looked directly at Mardee. "You can come, too," he said.

Mardee watched him saunter off and said, "He really has an appealing smile, don't you think?"

Lola nodded her head enthusiastically. "I like him," she said.

"Well," Mardee said with a touch of anxiety in her voice. "We'll have to check out Mr. Spangler. He's almost too charming to be true."

Mardee frowned and looked away from Lola. Just then she heard a child's voice saying, "Hello, Miss Mardee. I came to see you. I saw you dance."

Mardee looked down to see the perfect face of little Beth Corbin smiling up at her from the other side of her booth counter. "Well, hello, darling. Are you still here?"

Jeff walked up behind Beth at that moment. He had a relaxed smile on his face, and his eyes were bright with unspoken anticipation. "You were both so good up on that stage," he said. He turned to Lola and added, "Your voice is lovely, my dear."

Lola looked embarrassed, but also pleased. "Thank you," she murmured.

Jeff turned back to Mardee and said dryly, "You are a very expressive dancer, Mardee." Then his voice changed to a lower, huskier tone, and he continued, "Actually, you were absolutely gorgeous. I was so proud of you."

"Well, thank you, Jeff." Mardee tried to sound nonchalant, but she was keenly aware of the thrill of his compliment, and her eyes happily met his with obvious pleasure.

The spell of the moment was broken when a shrill voice called, "Elizabeth, Mommy is here."

Heather Corbin was walking briskly toward Mardee's booth. Beth turned around and saw her mother and instinctively moved closer to her father's side. "Come here," Heather said firmly. "Come to Mommy, dear."

As Heather took Beth's hand and pulled her away from her father, Jeff remarked, "The meeting must have lasted a long time."

"Well, there was much to discuss, and Father is the Chairman of the Board, you know, so I couldn't leave." Heather turned as she said, "Beth and I are going to the hotel. I'm sure she is very tired. You'll be coming, too." The last sentence was a command.

"Beth had a ball," Jeff said to the retreating back. "And she had a good dinner of hot dogs and apple pie."

Heather's shudder was visible as she reacted to the menu. She turned toward The Plaza Hotel.

"Are you staying at The Plaza tonight?" Mardee asked.

"Yes," Jeff answered. "We will have breakfast with Heather's father tomorrow morning. Then we'll head back for Santa Fe. By the way, did I see you talking to Jet Spangler?"

Mardee looked at Lola, and Lola smiled back at Mardee. "Yes," she said merrily. "We had a job offer. I don't know if he was sincere or not."

"I'm sure he was," Jeff said seriously. "Lola's voice is pure quality, and your dancing is breathtaking." Jeff looked off into the distance and added, "I didn't know you could dance like that, Mardee." He looked at her teasingly.

"Well, you knew I could do the Mexican Hat Dance, if I remember correctly," Mardee replied.

Jeff laughed spontaneously. Mardee knew he was thinking of the night at the Santa Fe Fiesta when they had danced together in The Plaza. I was so young, she thought, and so much in love with you. I was such a fool.

Mardee abruptly turned away from Jeff and said to Lola, "Let's pack up this stuff and head for home. I'm tired." The glitter and success of the evening had turned to salt and bitterness.

Jeff helped carry boxes to the car. I can't let him see these tears, Mardee admonished herself. She waved and smiled as Jeff turned toward the hotel, and she headed her car toward Santa Fe.

9

The heat of July and August did its best to stifle the active lives of Mardee and Lola. Even in the foothills of the mountains, the temperatures hovered around one hundred degrees, but the young women continued their busy schedules. Mardee worked at the office at least ten hours a day and then came home to change hurriedly and pick up Lola for their nightly stint at the Santa Fe Drama Company. They had gotten rolls in the new play and had practiced every night for a month. Now they were performing for the tourists who swarmed into Santa Fe in the summertime. Lola was singing in the chorus, and Mardee had a role as one of the minor characters, a girl named Mary. And she danced with a partner when Lola sang the sad song, *So Long Mary*. Both new actresses loved the theater and the performing. As Mardee's English teacher had said of her at the Loretta Academy, "She has such rapport with the audience. She has an amazing insight into human actions and reactions for one so young. She was born for the stage." Mardee knew the small role she played had a major impact on the play so she threw her whole being into the two hour performance. For a short while during the day her thoughts were only on her character, not on the battle field in France.

Lola loved every bit of show business, the costumes, the make-up, the chaos, and the rapport with her audience. Singing was easy for her, and she drank in the suggestions from the music director and knew her voice grew better with each performance. She was physically uncomfortable in the last stages of her pregnancy, but she wanted to sing until her labor pains started.

She had found her niche in life, and she planned to stay right there. She thanked God every night for bringing her to Santa Fe and to Jet Spangler and the theater. I suppose I should thank Ben Spencer and Mardee, too, she reminded herself.

Mardee scoured over the daily papers looking for war news. Of course, it was late by the time she read it. She knew the last German offensive had failed in the second battle of Marne, so the Allies must be starting another offensive, maybe a final one. She felt sure in her soul that Carter was fighting in these battles. She prayed for him all day long as she typed and performed her law office duties. She wrote him every night after she got home from the performance. Her last thought at night was of him, and he was her first thought in the morning when she opened her eyes to the new day.

Another reason Mardee knew Carter must be on the front lines was because the brief notes he wrote her were getting scarcer. He always apologized for not writing more often, but his excuse was, "We're very busy." He wrote once about being close to the artist's garden where the great master did his painting. "I'll bring you back here some time and take you there, if you'll learn to paint." She thought he must be referring to Monet's Garden. One time he described his captain: "A man who can smile and laugh in the face of adversity and death; truly a man of incalculable worth." His last note had stated, "When I come back here some day, I'll know I'm on consecrated ground." She didn't dare think about the things that were happening there which would make him feel it was "consecrated ground."

When the starlets rushed to the theater on the first Saturday in September, Mardee noticed that Lola's face appeared swollen. When she mentioned her observation, Lola tossed her head and said, "My feet are that way, too. It won't affect my singing." Nevertheless, Mardee watched Lola very carefully that evening and was relieved when she could take her home. Lola immediately fell into bed, complaining of back pains.

During the last Sunday performance Mardee noticed grimaces on the flushed face of Lola. After the performance, Lola answered quietly when

Mardee asked her how she felt, "Take me home and get the doctor. I think I've been having pains for two days."

"Why didn't you tell me?" Mardee asked anxiously.

"What could you have done?" Lola asked quietly. "Child birth has to run its course, and it sometimes takes quite a while. I've seen it happen with my stepmothers. But I think the pains are going to get serious now."

Mardee drove by Grant Street and picked up Addie Roberts and dropped Addie and Lola at her house. She told Addie to take care of the patient while she went to fetch the doctor. She knew Lola was in good hands.

Dr. Amble's home and office were on Lincoln Street and a light shone from his residence window. Mardee bounded out of the car and banged on the door. The doctor, a small man with spectacles on his nose and only a few wisps of grey hair on his head, promptly opened the door.

"Doctor," Mardee gasped, "it's Lola. She is ready to have her baby."

"I knew it would be soon," the doctor said calmly. "I'll get my bag."

When Mardee and Dr. Amble got back to the house, Addie greeted them at the door. "Her pains are very regular now," she informed the doctor. "I have hot water on."

Mardee gladly turned the responsibility of the birthing over to the doctor and Addie and went into the living room and collapsed into an easy chair. She had just closed her eyes gratefully when a horrendous scream penetrated her dazed senses and brought her to a stiff upright position. She jumped up and headed for the bedroom. She opened the door a crack but saw nothing to alarm her. The doctor stood calmly at the foot of the bed saying in an encouraging voice, "You're doing fine, Lola. Push hard when you feel the next pain coming on." Another wild scream suddenly split the air before Mardee got back to her chair.

"Oh, dear God," the frightened young woman gasped as she ran through the living room and out the front door. She didn't know where she was going. She just knew she had to get away from Lola's suffering. As she turned to head down the street, car lights suddenly shone in her eyes. She hastened over to the side of the road and waited for the car to pass. The car didn't pass, though. It stopped.

"Mardee?" a questioning voice called to her.

"Yes," Mardee said weakly.

"It's Jeff," the voice continued from the car.

Mardee walked slowly over to the side of the car. "Jeff?" she questioned.

Jeff jumped from the driver's side and ran around to open the door for Mardee. "Can I take you some place? Where were you going?" Jeff held the car door open and looked at Mardee with concern on his face.

"I don't know," Mardee answered. "Just away. Lola is having her baby."

"Oh," Jeff said understandingly. "I see. Rough time?"

"It sounds like it," Mardee said in a tremulous voice.

Jeff put a supporting arm around Mardee. "Get in," he said kindly. "We'll go back to the house and see how she's doing."

Mardee heaved a sigh of relief as she leaned her head back on the car seat. She was thankful that Jeff had appeared when she needed him, but she vaguely wondered why he was here in this neighborhood at this time. It doesn't matter, she thought. He's here, that's the important thing.

Jeff stopped the car in front of the house and said, "I'll run in and see how she is doing. Do you want to stay here?"

"Yes," Mardee said apologetically. "I should go in, but..."

"That's fine," Jeff said as he opened his door. "I'll be back shortly."

Mardee crunched her trembling body into her seat and felt relieved that she didn't hear any screams. She closed her eyes and tried to relax. I don't know if I could go through this, she thought. I don't think I ever want to try having a baby. The sound of quick steps interrupted her tumultuous thoughts, and Jeff opened the door on the other side and quickly pushed himself in behind the wheel.

"She's coming along," he said. "Progress is slow because it's her first baby. Her pelvic muscles are strong, and they are not giving enough to let the baby through. It will take time."

"How much time?" Mardee asked nervously.

"Two more hours should do it," Jeff looked into Mardee's distraught face and added, "She'll be all right. Don't worry." He impulsively took one of her hands and held it tightly.

Mardee looked into his face and felt somewhat reassured. "You're more experienced in this type of happening than I," she deducted.

"Only a little," he said. "Beth was born in a hospital in Washington, DC. I didn't see Heather from the time I took her to the hospital until the baby was born two hours later. I was in a waiting room far away from the action."

"That is where I would want to be," Mardee said firmly.

Jeff held Mardee's hand in silence for a few minutes, and then he said, "Would you like to go to the restaurant in the La Fonda and have a cool drink and relax? We haven't had a chance to visit since I came back. Nothing is going to happen here for a while."

Getting away from this house sounded very appealing to Mardee right now. "Thanks, Jeff," she said appreciatively. "I would like that."

The hotel was only a short distance away, and Mardee and Jeff were soon going through the huge wooden doors and past the lobby to the restaurant. Mardee sank down gratefully into the comfortably cushioned booth. There were few patrons there at this time of night, and a Spanish waitress was at their table immediately.

"Bring us coffee," Jeff said with a smile. "And how about a piece of pie, Mardee? They have wonderful coconut pies here."

Mardee suddenly realized she was hungry. She and Lola hadn't had time to eat before they left for the theater. "That sounds wonderful," she said happily. "And, could I have a sandwich? Maybe I got so scared because I'm so hungry." She looked at Jeff appealingly.

Jeff turned his charms on the waitress and said, "I know it is late, but would you make a plate for this lady with whatever you have left in the kitchen? Macaroni and cheese with a few beans would be great. And, of course, the coconut pie for dessert."

The waitress left, and Mardee smiled at Jeff gratefully. "You came along at the right time tonight. I don't know what I would have done. Usually I don't act like a hysterical woman."

"You're entitled just this once," Jeff said firmly. "Birth is a very serious matter."

"What were you doing riding around at this time of night?" Mardee asked.

"I was just out to get a little night air," Jeff said vaguely.

At that moment the waitress brought their coffee, and Mardee poured sugar and cream in her cup generously. "I only drink it for the sugar and cream," she explained.

Jeff smiled and took a sip of his black coffee. "You're not a true coffee lover," he said. He leaned comfortably back against the soft back of the booth and continued, "We went to the theater last night and watched the play. You do very well in your part, and Lola's voice is breathtaking."

"Thanks," Mardee said between sips of the hot liquid. "Another girl is lined up to take Lola's place for the next two weeks, so I'm glad you saw the play with Lola doing the singing."

"I'm glad she's taking some time off," Jeff said.

"You should have come back stage and visited with us," Mardee said.

"I would have liked to do just that," Jeff said. After a little hesitation, he added, "Heather didn't approve of that idea."

"Why?" Mardee asked innocently. "Does she know we are old friends?"

"I have told her that," Jeff answered quickly, "but Heather is a little paranoid along with being very bright. She seems to sense there may have been more to the relationship."

"Are you saying she is jealous of me?" Mardee looked straight into Jeff's eyes and demanded an honest answer.

Jeff glanced away quickly and watched the waitress bringing a tray of food for them. "Wonderful," Jeff remarked as he saw the plate of roast beef, potatoes, and chili beans set in front of Mardee. "She needs a glass of milk also," he directed the waitress.

The waitress nodded her head and was gone, and Mardee started on her food with dedication. "This is so good," she said. "I think I'm starved. Come to think of it, I worked through lunch time. I usually run down to The Plaza and get an enchilada, but there just wasn't time."

"Poor baby," Jeff said with mock concern. "What would you do without me?"

Mardee felt her old feistiness returning as she gulped the food down. "I would probably do very well without you," she said between bites. "Actually, I have done very well without you."

"I know," Jeff said quickly. "I'm sorry I asked you that question. It wasn't really a serious question."

Mardee pointed her fork at Jeff and jabbed the air. "As I was asking, is your wife jealous of me?"

"Probably," Jeff answered. "She's jealous of every woman as far as I'm concerned. If she were here, she'd be jealous of this waitress because I smiled at her. She's a very insecure woman. I don't know why, because I've never given her any cause to worry about other women."

"That's too bad," Mardee said, instantly feeling sorry for both Heather and Jeff.

"I know," Jeff said with a sad shake of his head. "It's not a good situation for either of us. But Beth is the one I really worry about. I think she's jealous of mine and Beth's relationship. Do you think that's normal? Shouldn't a father love his daughter?"

"Absolutely," Mardee said decisively. "I don't know what I would have done without the love of my father. I'm sure it's very important for a daughter to know her father loves her unequivocally."

"Well, I do," Jeff said nodding his head vigorously. "She's the light of my life."

"She's a doll," Mardee said with a soft smile.

The waitress brought Mardee's pie and refilled the coffee cups. Jeff took a careful sip and asked, "What about your life, Mardee? How is your marriage?"

Mardee chewed appreciatively on a big bite of her pie and answered, "I married the best man in the world, Jeff. He loves me and understands me. He gives me whatever I want, but I don't take advantage of that weakness. I was raised practically and frugally. You know Ben Spencer and Mother Spencer." She paused and smiled at Jeff. He returned her smile and winked. "He's also a very bright and promising attorney," Mardee continued. "He's six feet four inches tall and weighs over two hundred pounds. I think he could wrestle a bull. But he's a very gentle man. I call him my gentle giant. He's got a thriving law business started. His partner, Will, and I are keeping it going. I have two more courses to finish, and I'll have my law degree by Christmas. Then I'll be a partner in the firm. That's about it as far as I'm concerned." Mardee said and continued with her pie.

"He's quite a man, it sounds like," Jeff said, and his voice sounded a little strained. "I'm happy for you. You deserve a good man." He was silent a moment as his eyes looked contemplatively away. Then he returned his gaze to Mardee and said, "I heard you say he loves you, but I didn't hear you say that you love him. Do you Mardee?" His eyes were boring into hers demandingly.

"Of course, I love him," Mardee said defensively. "What's not to love? He's the best." Mardee put her fork down. Suddenly her pie didn't look or taste so delicious. She jumped up. "I'm ready to go," she announced. "We'd better check on Lola."

Jeff rose to leave. There was a speculatively smile on his face. He didn't need to ask any more questions. He had his answer.

When Jeff and Mardee walked into the house a few minutes later, a sense of peace and quietness had replaced the former chaos. Addie met them at the door and said, "The baby is here. He's a big healthy boy. He weighs over nine pounds, and it was a hard birth, but mother and baby are fine."

"Thank God," Mardee said joyfully. "Can I see them?"

"In just a few minutes. The doctor is still working over her. She lost a lot of blood." Addie disappeared back into the bedroom.

"Isn't that wonderful?" Mardee exclaimed to Jeff. "A boy! That's what she wanted."

"Having a boy would be wonderful," Jeff said in a listless voice.

Mardee perceived immediately that Jeff would like another child, a boy, but his wife wouldn't go along with his wishes. She must be such a selfish, self-centered person, she thought. The picture Jeff had drawn for her tonight wasn't an attractive one. Jeff and Mardee stood silently, each wrapped in their own thoughts.

Dr. Amble came out at that moment, drying his hands on a towel. "You may go in now," he said. "But don't talk to her very long. She is very tired. She must have her rest now, and after a few days she'll be fine. I'll drop by to see her tomorrow and every day for a while, to make sure she and the little one are doing all right."

Mardee started in the bedroom door, but she turned and asked Jeff, "Would you take Doctor Amble home? That would be a big help."

"Of course," Jeff said affably. "Pack your bag, doctor, and I'll drop you off on my way home."

Mardee stepped quietly to Lola's bedside. The new mother lay there like a crumpled rose on her pillow. Her cheeks were pallid and her long eyelashes splashed across her cheeks like the broken wings of a bird. In contrast, the baby lay by her side in all his rosy good health. Mardee bent closer to look at him, and Lola's eyelids fluttered. Her lips formed a beatific smile, and she murmured, "Did you see the baby?"

"Tears came to Mardee's eyes, and she whispered, "He's gorgeous." His eyes opened on cue, and she said, "Hello, little Robbie Blue Eyes. We love you already."

Lola smiled and closed her eyes again as did her baby. "Good job, Lola," Mardee whispered. "Go to sleep. I'll see you tomorrow."

Addie was sitting in a chair on the other side of the bed. "I'll stay with her and the baby tonight," she whispered. "You go on to bed yourself, and I'll make sure everything is all right."

Mardee blew Addie a kiss and tiptoed out of the room. She found her way to her dark bedroom and fell down on the top of the bed still in her clothes. She knew she was too tired to change into her night gown. She offered a prayer of thanksgiving to God for the well-being of Lola and her baby, and then she immediately drifted off into an exhausted dreamless sleep.

10

Mardee was awakened the next morning by a soft tapping on her bedroom door. She roused up and called out sleepily, "Come in."

Addie stuck her head in and said softly, "Lola is bathed and nursing her baby. When she finishes, feed her some breakfast. Hot cereal and juice would be good for her. I'm going home to get some sleep. I'll be back to check on her this evening."

"Oh, I'm sorry," Mardee said as she threw the covers back. "I should be up."

"Everything is fine," Addie assured her with a smile. "Lola feels much better, and the baby is eating like a little pig. He's a grand boy."

Mardee threw on a robe and walked with Addie to Lola's bedroom. She was propped up on pillows while she gazed down lovingly at her new son. She looked up at Mardee with contentment shining in her soft brown eyes. "Isn't he beautiful?" she asked softly.

Mardee scrutinized the tiny piece of new humanity. She hadn't seen many babies, but she didn't think she would describe him as beautiful. His face was red and wrinkled, and his nose was flat. His eyes were tightly closed, and the intent look on his face gave a hint as to the seriousness of his pursuit of food. Soft black hair covered his head.

"He has your hair," Mardee observed.

"His eyes are blue," Lola said smugly.

"Like his father's?" Mardee asked quietly.

Lola looked directly into Mardee's questioning face and said, "Yes. I

71

promised you I would tell you about his father." She paused and said after taking a deep breath. "He worked at the mill for Mr. Spencer for a few months. I made a mistake, Mardee. After he found out I was in the family way, he left, and I never heard from him."

"I'm sorry," Mardee said as tears came to her eyes. "We all make mistakes, but I'm not really saying this baby is a mistake." She took one of the tiny hands, and he grasped her fingers tightly. "He's so strong," she exclaimed.

"His father was a tall handsome man," Lola said with a sad smile. "I was accustomed to your brothers, Mardee. They were honest and never lied to me. I believed everything he told me. He said we would get married, but he left."

"Do you know where he went?"

Lola shook her head. "No, and I'm sure he will never come back. Floyd gave him the beating of his life and sent him packing. Floyd took it very hard, Mardee. Perhaps he cared for me, but I thought of him as a brother. Anyway, he's the reason the baby is named Robert, for Floyd."

Mardee nodded her head slowly. "Yes, his name is Robert Floyd."

"He's a good man," Lola said. "That's when he joined the Army."

Mardee had wondered why Floyd left her father when he needed him so much in his lumber business. Now I know, she thought.

Addie suddenly broke the silence after Lola's remarks. "I must go. I called Jeff for a ride, and he just drove up. Just rest and eat, Lola. You'll soon feel your strength coming back."

Jeff appeared at the front door. "May I come in?" he called.

Mardee ran to the door and opened it. "I'm ready to go," Addie said as she came out of the bedroom.

"Could I take a look at the baby?" Jeff asked.

"Of course," Mardee said as she led the way.

Jeff stood by the side of the bed with his hat in his hand and looked tenderly down at mother and baby. Mardee glanced at his face. She remembered their conversation of the night before when he had told her his wife refused to have the son he wanted. There were tears in his eyes. She felt a momentary pang of compassion for him. Then she silently remembered the reason he had married Heather. For his own ambition. He had thought Heather's father, who was then the lieutenant governor, would be influential in helping him accomplish his political dreams. Apparently nothing was working out for him. He's getting what he deserves, she told herself, but nevertheless, her heart ached for him.

"You'd better take Addie home," she said softly. "She's very tired. And could you stop by the office and tell Will I won't be in today?"

"Sure," Jeff said. "I'll check on you later," he assured Lola. "Just call Uncle Jeff if you need anything."

The baby had finished eating, and Mardee lifted him carefully and put him over her shoulder as she gently patted his back. He burped quickly, and she put him in the little bed Addie had found in her attic for them to use. She fluffed Lola's pillows and instructed her to relax and rest. "I can do that," Lola said gratefully.

"Do you feel all right?" Mardee asked curiously. "After all, that was quite an ordeal."

"I feel wonderful," Lola said as she snuggled into her pillows.

She must not remember much about last night, Mardee thought as she tiptoed out of the room. How could she feel wonderful after what she's been through?

She had no time to debate that question, though, because another visitor was at the door. Jet stood there looking embarrassed and clutching a huge bouquet of flowers. "I'm sorry I'm here so early," he apologized. "But the whole cast wanted Lola to have these flowers."

"How pretty," Mardee said as she took the flowers. "You went out and picked wild flowers," she said as she noticed the bright red-orange Indian paint brushes among the paler colored blossoms.

Jet ducked his head, and his face turned fiery red. His usual jaunty aplomb seemed shattered, and he looked like an unsure little boy. "I...we thought these would brighten up her room." He shuffled his feet and asked anxiously, "How is she doing?"

"Wonderful," Mardee said, "anyway that's the word she uses to describe how she feels."

Jet looked relieved and turned to go. "I've got to get to practice," he mumbled.

"Come back tomorrow after she's stronger, and you can see her and the baby," Mardee called after him. That's interesting, she thought as she turned to find a vase for the flowers. The dapper Mr. Spangler seems to be rather discombobulated.

Mardee hastened to fix Lola's breakfast and admonished her to eat the oatmeal so she could make some milk for the baby. She had just changed from her robe when Lola had another visitor. "I can't believe this," she grumbled aloud.

Mardee opened the door to Jorje Gonzales. "Jorje!" she said in obvious surprise. "What are you doing here?"

"I brought you some fresh milk from the store," he said in perfect English. "I thought the new mother might need it."

"You knew Lola had her baby last night? How did you know? I didn't even know you knew Lola."

"Jeff told me," he answered her first question. "I know Lola because she comes to buy groceries at the store."

"Oh, I suppose so," Mardee said as she understood the connection. "Thank you for the milk. We can use it. And I'll tell Lola you brought it. She's doing fine and can have visitors by tomorrow."

"I cannot visit," Jorje hastily explained. "I will be working. But I deliver groceries on this street this morning, so I can stop here. Please tell her I'm happy for her. And, the baby? He is a boy and is healthy?"

"Oh yes," Mardee assured him. "He's a big boy and hungry already."

Jorje smiled, and his classic Spanish features conveyed his relief. "I'm glad she is all right. Now I must go back to work."

Mardee watched Jorje walk away with purposeful steps. The young boy who had come to her and asked her to teach him simple arithmetic so he could advance in his job at the Santa Fe Mercantile was now a handsome young man who had worked his way into the confidence of his boss and was also the co-manager of the store. I'm so proud of you, Jorje, she thought. I hope the girls do as well. Mardee had befriended the family many times, and she prayed that his sisters, who were developing into beautiful girls, would avoid the many pitfalls of pretty señoritas in Santa Fe. I must check on them, she reminded herself. I saw them walking and laughing in The Plaza one evening when it was too late for them to be out.

Mardee sat down at the kitchen table to have a cup of tea and eat a cinnamon roll. Mother Spencer taught Lola to cook well, she thought as she chewed on the delicious treat. I think I could still make them myself, but I can't seem to find the time. Lucky I have Lola here.

Then Mardee's thoughts zeroed in on Carter. Usually he was the first thing on her mind in the morning. "Sorry, darling," she whispered. "Lola's baby pushed you back for a while."

All the stories in the newspapers told of fierce fighting going on in France with the American Army. They also inferred this might be a final offensive that would end the war. You've got to get home, sweetheart, she thought. My life is so different with you gone. I need you so much. She put her head down on her hands and thought of the law firm and its responsibilities. We're doing fine, she realized, but I'll be starting back to school in a week. I can't be in the office and in school, too. How can Will do all the work? I must get some help for him.

And now Lola has a baby, Mardee's thoughts continued. We don't know anything about babies. How are we going to take care of him? Thank goodness Addie will help us.

Mardee lifted her head and took a sip of the hot tea. "I wish you were here to talk to me, Mother Spencer," she said as her thoughts went to her stepmother. You have such a way of cutting through life's complications and emphasizing the right path to follow. You just think of a verse in the Bible that tells you what to do." She closed her eyes and suddenly one of her own favorite verses flashed into her mind, "The path of the just is as a shining light that shineth more and more unto the perfect day."

"Dear God, be with me and be with Carter," she prayed. "Bring him through this terrible war and back safely to me. And help me stay the course so I can be worthy of the perfect day when Carter comes home." The demanding cry of little Robbie penetrated her thoughts, and she ran to the bedroom to take care of this newest responsibility.

11

Mardee went back to work, and made arrangements for Raquel Riley to come and stay with Lola and the new baby for a few days. Addie couldn't continue to spend time there since she had her piano students and her boarders.

"I'd rather be here," Addie said as she bathed Robbie. She patted sweet smelling baby powder all over his plump little body and diapered him. She checked the naval area and put olive oil on the dried remnant of the naval cord. Then she wrapped a protective cloth band tightly around the stomach area and secured it with two large safety pins. After she pulled the soft flannel gown over the baby's head she murmured, "Now to keep your little feet and legs warm." She encased his legs in long white stockings and attached them to the diaper with big pins. "There you go, little dumpling," she concluded as she held the baby tight to her breast momentarily and then took him to his mother

"What were you saying, Addie?" Lola asked as she took the baby. "I heard you talking to the baby."

"I was telling him how much I hate to leave him," Addie said with a chuckle. "It has been such a treat taking care of him."

"He will miss you," Lola said as she positioned the baby to her breast to let him nurse.. "Ouch!" she groaned as he hungrily latched onto the nipple and started sucking with vigor. "How long will I be so sore?" she asked between clenched teeth.

"Not long," Addie said comfortingly. "Your body will adjust quickly."

"Hello," came a cheerful voice from the other room. "It's Raquel. I just came in. Angela and I are moving in with you."

Addie went to greet Raquel. She stood there holding Angela in one arm and a suitcase in the other. Her father stood beside her carrying a large box. "Come on in," Addie said quickly. "Bring your things in Mardee's bedroom. She said that is where you will stay. How are you, Mr. Sanchez?"

Miguel Sanchez smiled broadly and bowed his head slightly. "Bien, Señora, gracias. I come to see the new niño."

Raquel headed for Mardee's room and her father followed. She set down her little girl and the suitcase with a sigh of relief. After they all took a quick look at the new baby, Raquel directed, "Tell your abuelo bye, bye, Angela."

"Bye, bye, nieta," Miguel said as adoration for his little granddaughter softened his weatherworn face.

"You come and get me in one week, Papa. OK?"

"Si, si," Miguel said with assurance. "I will be here."

Miguel drove off, and Raquel went to the bedroom to unpack and arrange her room for her stay. Angela remained in the bedroom watching the baby with big eyes. "Do you like him?" Lola asked as she looked at her son tenderly.

"Oh yes," Angela said decisively. "But he is very little."

"He will grow," Lola said. "Someday he will be big like you."

"But not as big as me," Angela announced. .

"Someday he will," Lola said with a smile.

"But not now," Angela persisted.

Suddenly there was a knock on the front door. "Run and open the front door, Angela," Lola directed.

Angela did as she was told and opened the door to a young gentleman. "Hello," she said shyly as she looked up at the visitor. She put a finger in her mouth, but her eyes held steady in her gaze.

Raquel came at that moment and stood behind her daughter. "Hello George," she said with a smile. "Mardee's not here, and I'm taking care of

Lola and the baby. What brings you away from the store?"

George extended a brown sack toward Raquel. "Here are fresh apples from the Española orchards. I thought maybe Lola would enjoy some fresh fruit."

Raquel took the apples. "I'm sure we will all enjoy them. Please come in." She beamed at the man with whom she often visited when she came to Santa Fe to get groceries

Jorje stood uncertainly inside the doorway. Lola called from her bedroom, "Bring Jorje in so he can see the baby."

"Come along," Raquel motioned to Jorje. He walked uncertainly behind her.

Raquel took the baby, who was sleeping peacefully after nursing, and held him toward Jorje for his inspection. The baby snuffled gently and blinked his eyes briefly. Jorje gazed at the small bundle incredulously and involuntarily took a step backwards.

"He won't bite you," Raquel admonished him. "Isn't he a fine boy?"

"Oh yes!" Jorje said with a voice full of embarrassed animation. "He is very fine."

After a moment Lola said, breaking an uncomfortable silence now starting to dominate the visit, "Did I hear you say you had brought apples? Thank you for the apples."

Jorje suddenly spoke in a staccato voice. "Yes, Lola, I brought you some fresh apples. I hope you enjoy them. Now I must go to work." Jorje turned decisively around to leave.

Lola smiled at Raquel and then called to Jorje's back "Thank you so much, George. You are so kind. Please come back."

Raquel heard the front door open and close. She laid the baby in his bed and turned to Lola with a teasing smile. "Is he an admirer?"

"Oh no," Lola said with a shrug of her shoulders. "He's just a good friend. Mardee has known him ever since she came to Santa Fe. She takes quite an interest in George and his sisters. George is like a brother to both of us."

"I doubt he thinks of you as a sister," Raquel said with certainty as she turned to leave the bedroom. "I must get to that tub of diapers Addie has soaking," she explained. .

Raquel washed the diapers and hung them out to dry in the hot southwestern sun. Angela tripped merrily around under the flapping clothes and sang a tuneless song. The diapers look so pretty and white, she thought as she watched the clothes and Angela dance gracefully in the light wind. I'll fix some lunch for Lola, and then I'll put Angela down for a nap, and maybe I can get some rest, too, she reasoned.

But Raquel had barely gone back in the house when another visitor arrived. A tall dapper fellow stood at the doorway smiling engagingly. "Hello," he called. "I've come to check on the new mother and her son." Raquel hurried to open the door, and the man continued, "I'm Jetson Spangler, the director at the theater."

Raquel looked impressed and led the visitor to the bedroom. Lola lay on her side facing away from the door. "She must be asleep," Raquel whispered.

But Lola had heard the noise and suddenly raised her head and looked over her back. Her eyes met those of her visitor, and her pale face turned red with a rosy blush. Jet walked over to her bed and took the hand she stretched toward him. "I didn't come before, dear," he said softly. "I wanted to wait until you felt stronger."

"I'm so glad you are here, Jet." Lola exclaimed. "I've missed you."

"You've missed my complaining and demanding," Jet said in a merry voice. Then, more seriously, he continued, "We've missed you at the production. No one can do your part or sing as you do."

"I'm sure Estelle is doing fine," Lola said.

"I have news for you," Jet said. "A friend of mine who works in New York City on Broadway is coming through here on his way to Hollywood in the near future. I've told him about you. He wants to hear you sing and see you perform."

"Really?" Lola asked in a reverential voice. "He wants to see me?"

"Someone from Broadway wants to see and hear you, little Lola Tompkins. We may have to change your name, darling. How would you like to be Lola Lee?"

Lola shook her head. Slowly she said, "Things are happening too fast. I can't think right now."

"He won't be here for a while. You don't have to think about it now. I just mainly wanted to see you." Jet quickly changed the subject of their conversation. "May I see the boy?"

"He's over here," Raquel said quickly "He's asleep, but you can tiptoe over here and see him." She led the way to the baby's crib.

Jet glanced down at the baby with a perfunctory look and turned away quickly. He walked back to the other side of the bed and took both of Lola's hands. "I've got to run, darling. You know, busy, busy. You look as if you are doing very well. The roses in your cheeks are coming back. You'll be returning to work soon?"

"Oh yes," Lola said in a breathy voice. "I can't wait to be back. Addie has said she will take care of the baby for me."

"Good," Jet said. "I'm going to start a new production soon. I'm thinking about doing 'Carmen,' and I may want you to do the main part. You might have to have some singing classes in the meantime. What do you think of that?"

"Wonderful," Lola said. There were stars in her expressive brown eyes.

Jet smiled at Raquel and told her he was happy to have met her, and then he was out of the bedroom and through the living room with quick steps. When the front door closed, Raquel said to Lola, "I can see you like Mr. Spangler. He must be a good director."

"Oh yes!" Lola said excitedly. "He's wonderful."

Raquel turned abruptly and left the room. "I'll put Angela down for a nap, and I'll peel an apple for you and bring it to you for a snack." Quietly, she murmured. "I prefer George who brings you apples, but his apples probably aren't going to measure up to the promises of the dashing Jetson Spangler."

Mardee came home just as the red-gold sun was dropping down behind the mountains to the west. She was getting as much work done as possible before she started to school the next week. She was very tired and she was anxious at the thought of leaving Will alone in the office. She would have classes on Mondays and Wednesdays and could be in the office Thursdays, Fridays, and Saturdays. But was that enough time to keep the office running smoothly? More clients were walking into the law firm every day. Many mines were starting up in the mountains around Tererro, Madrid, and Cerrillos, and there were unending questions about rights and claims and ownership. She knew that she and Will were becoming the recognized legal experts in the mining field. Their services were in demand in this developing industry.

Raquel was sitting in an easy chair on the patio when Mardee parked in front of the house. She was fanning the evening heat away from her face and eating an apple. "How did it go today?" Mardee asked as she dropped down into another chair.

"Fine," Raquel said. "Supper is over with, and everyone is in bed and asleep, but me. Have an apple. George brought them today. I think bringing apples was just an excuse to see Lola. Is there something going on there?"

Mardee sighed and answered, "Not as far as Lola is concerned, but Jorje is smitten. I feel bad for him. He's a fine young man who works hard and will make something out of himself, but he's too slow and unexciting for Lola." Mardee reached for an apple in a bowl on the patio table.

"Her director was also here," Raquel said, and the tone of her voice conveyed her lack of enthusiasm for this visitor. "Lola was all smiles for him."

"Jetson Spangler? Oh yes, Lola likes him." Mardee leaned back in her chair and closed her eyes. The apple lay untouched in her lap.

"You're very tired," Raquel observed. "I'll bring you a plate of food out here. Just sit still," she ordered as Mardee started to stir.

Raquel returned shortly with a bowl of green chili stew and a fresh tortilla. The sight of food brought Mardee to life, and she started eating with gusto. "I didn't realize how hungry I am," she said between bites. "I took a sandwich to work for lunch, but it's been a long time since noon."

Raquel brought Mardee a baked apple and a glass of milk to finish off her meal. "This apple is delicious," she said. "How do you cook it?"

"Cut the core out and fill it with sugar and cinnamon and butter. Put a little water, corn starch, and vanilla in the bottom of the pan."

"Sounds easy enough," Mardee commented. "But the simple things are always the best."

Mardee finished eating and picked up her dishes to carry into the kitchen. "You're a good cook, Raquel, but did you ever think of doing anything outside the home? You were a good student in school." An idea was beginning to formulate in Mardee's brain.

"I feel I'm needed at home," Raquel replied. "I keep the ranch books for Papa."

"Did you take typing?" Mardee asked.

"Yes, I'm a good typist, but I don't do much of it anymore."

Raquel held the door open and Mardee set her dishes down on the counter. "Don't worry about them tonight," she instructed Raquel. "They'll wait until morning." She turned and faced Raquel and said, "Raquel, you do realize we are in a war and everyone has to pitch in and help out while so many of our men are fighting overseas, don't you?"

"Yes," Raquel answered hesitantly. "What do you mean?"

"I mean that my husband is in a trench fighting in France, and I'm trying to go to school and keep his law firm going at the same time. I'm afraid I can't get it all done, Raquel. Could you possibly work in the office three days a week while I'm in school? Will needs a secretary badly."

Raquel merely looked at Mardee, and no words came out of her mouth. Finally, her mouth opened and she mumbled a few words. "I don't know..."

"Well, think about it," Mardee said impatiently. "I'm sure you could learn to be a legal secretary. You would learn the job while you get paid for working. I'm sure your mother would take care of Angela for three days a week."

"Well, I could use the money. The ranch isn't doing too well right now because of the drought," Raquel conceded.

"You'd be perfect," Mardee said quickly. "You would be an asset to the office. Besides typing and keeping the books, you could converse with the Spanish speaking people. Will can't do that very well when I'm not there. And I'm sure we could make it worth your time to do the job."

"I'd have to learn to drive," Raquel said as if talking to herself. "Do you think I could drive a car?"

"Of course, you can," Mardee said with assurance. "Remember the speeches you've heard me give about women being able to do anything if they just try? You signed the Suffrage Petition. Now you have to prove you truly believe what you profess to believe."

"I do believe in equal rights for women," Raquel said defensively.

"Then you can help out during this wartime manpower crunch," Mardee said firmly. "We'll talk more about this later. Anyway, for now I don't want to deter you from your present job of running this household and being a nurse." Mardee impulsively threw her arms around Raquel's shoulders. "I appreciate you so much. I'm going to write Carter a letter tonight and tell him what a help you are to me and to Lola and the baby. I just couldn't do it all by myself. God bless you, dear friend."

Raquel retired to Mardee's bedroom to sleep with Angela. Mardee spread her blanket and pillow on her divan and tiredly pulled another blanket over her. She quickly kicked it off, but later in the night she knew she would need it after the heat of the day abated. She said a short prayer for Carter and thanked God for giving her the idea of hiring Raquel in the office. She won't sleep much tonight, she thought. She'll be thinking about this job and wrestling with her doubts about being able to do this kind of work. "I know you can do it, Raquel," she murmured and closed her eyes and was instantly asleep.

12

Mardee finished posting figures in the law accounts ledger with finality. "That's done," she said aloud. "Everything is done for today." She got up from her desk and walked briskly into Will's office.

Will sat behind his desk, his head bowed over a brief. He didn't look up immediately, but finished reading the page and carefully turned it. "Yes?" he asked finally.

"Will, I appreciate all your hard work," Mardee said in a sincere voice. "The law firm is doing well, mainly thanks to you. But, perhaps Carter will be back soon. The paper today reports that the Allies have won the Battle of Marne, so our men should be coming home before too long, unless he has been one of the unlucky ones, God forbid, and was hurt in the last battle.. The report is of many killed and wounded." Mardee took a deep breath as if to clear the apprehension from her mind.

Will's gentle gray eyes mirrored concern. "He's going to come home," he said quietly. "We must have faith, Mardee."

Mardee concentrated her attention on this mild man who lived and worked so unobtrusively. She knew he had a wife, but she'd never met her. He never mentioned children. Who are you, really, Will Cabot? she wondered. Besides being a conscientious worker, who are you? Aloud, she said, "I hope you are right. I pray you are right." Mardee pulled a chair up close to the desk. "We need to have a talk, Will."

Will nodded his head and pushed his papers aside. "Of course, Mardee."

"You know I am starting back to school next week. I will be able to help out only on Thursdays and Fridays and weekends. I have made arrangements for Raquel Riley to come in and work the first part of the week when I'm not here. Raquel is a young woman with whom I attended school at The Academy. She's very capable, but she has been only a housewife and mother for a few years. Her typing skills will come back fast, though. She has had a bookkeeping course in school, and I'll bring her down tomorrow after church and show her how we do our accounts. We can afford to start her out at a minimal wage. I hope you are agreeable to this plan."

The bland expression on Will's face didn't change, but he nodded his head affirmatively. "That sounds fine to me."

"Very well," Mardee said, nodding her head also. "She will report for work on Monday morning."

As Mardee rose from her chair signaling an end to their meeting, Will said, glancing at his watch, "I think I will go home now. Good luck in your schooling."

"This finishes me up, you know," Mardee said cheerily. "I'll be a full-fledged lawyer in a few months." She tripped out of Will's office on her smart high-heeled pumps, softly singing the words to the song, "Over There." "'And we won't come back till it's over, over there,'" she finished the verse and called back to Will, "Of course, I have to pass my bar test, you know."

Mardee sat down to read the paper more thoroughly. She heard Will say, "Good day, Mardee," and the door closed.

Mardee had just folded up the paper and leaned back in her chair to relax a moment before she headed for home when she heard the door open again. "Did you forget something?" she called, thinking Will had returned.

"Yes," came the strident answer. "I forgot to visit you today." A masculine figure appeared in her door, and Jeff Corbin stood there beaming at her with a mischievous smile on his face.

Mardee returned his infectious good humor with a grin and a flippant remark. "As you have forgotten to visit me for many days. How come I rate today?"

86

"May I sit a while?" Jeff asked as he pulled up a chair to face her. His expression turned serious, and he said, "Actually, I came to tell you some news that might interest you."

"Well, tell me, by all means," Mardee said in a light voice.

"You have heard of Jeanette Reynolds, the congresswoman from Montana?"

"Certainly," Mardee replied in a more serious tone. "I have kept up with her career. She is the first woman elected to the U. S. Congress, you know. That is quite an honor."

"Indeed," Jeff said. "Well, you might just be interested to know that she will be visiting here in Santa Fe for a few days."

"I certainly am interested," Mardee said as her face colored with rosy animation. "You know, she is a strong advocate of women's rights."

"Oh yes, I know all about that," Jeff said. "She's also a pacifist and voted against entering the war. I met the woman in Washington, DC. She and Heather became good friends. She will be staying in our home while she is here."

"I am impressed," Mardee said in a teasingly stilted tone of voice. "The noted Jeanette Reynolds, a guest in your home." Mardee tapped her fingers on her desk and looked off into space, her eyes thoughtful. "You know," she said slowly, "I'm planning one more suffrage rally before I send all my petitions to Washington. Maybe I could do it while she is here and invite her to be a guest speaker." Mardee turned her eyes back to Jeff, and they were sparkling with anticipation.

"She is coming on November tenth," Jeff said. "If you planned something about that time, I'm sure she would be pleased to be present. In fact, I would exert my influence in that direction."

"Oh Jeff, would you really?"

"Your childlike enthusiasm never ceases to amaze me, Mardee. I can promise you that Jeanette Reynolds will attend your rally. You have my word."

"The word of Jeff Corbin I will accept, in my childlike way," Mardee said primly.

"What do you hear from your husband?" Jeff asked. "The war news sounds better."

"Yes, thank God. I hope he will be returning home soon."

"I'm sure it has been tough for you while he's been away," Jeff sympathized. "And, you've had other complications," he added. "How are the new mother and baby doing?"

"Fine," Mardee answered. "The baby is very good and only sleeps, eats, and grows. Lola will soon be back at the theater. Her director has big plans for her. She may have a starring roll in the next play."

"She is a very talented girl," Jeff said. "But what about you? Have you given up your acting and dancing aspirations? You are very talented, also."

"Thank you, but I'm going to concentrate in another direction now. You can't do everything, you know. I've done my last performance at the Santa Fe Drama Company."

"Perhaps when your husband gets back and you're not needed so much in the office, you can go back," Jeff suggested.

"I doubt it," Mardee said. "It's back to law school for me now, and I'll be finished by Christmas. Then my name goes up on the sign outside."

"Well," I'm glad things are going so well for you." Jeff looked away quickly, but Mardee caught a hint of sadness in his eyes.

"How are things going for you?" she asked.

"Well, slow, to say the least. I'm having trouble building a law firm from the ground. I've been gone so long from Santa Fe that most people have forgotten me. And there's a new governor with whom I have no influence."

"And a new lieutenant governor," Mardee added, remembering the part the former lieutenant governor had played in Jeff's rejection of her. He had chosen to marry Heather, thinking her father would help him with his political ambitions. Obviously, his plan hadn't worked out so well. But she was immediately sorry for her remark as she looked into Jeff's downcast face. "It takes a while to get a law firm established," she added. "Will and I are finally getting this one going, but it has not been easy."

"I try to explain that to Heather, but she has no patience. She isn't happy with our situation here." Jeff sighed and Mardee noticed the lines on his forehead and the gray in his blonde mustache. The thought of the gallant Jeff Corbin growing old was one she could not accept.

"I'm sorry," Mardee said with genuine sincerity. Even though Jeff had not treated her well, it was not her disposition to revel in someone's travesty.

"I'm thinking perhaps I should try to get in with an established firm," Jeff said. "But I don't think Heather would like the idea of me not having my own law business. It's very important for her to keep up the appearance of success and wealth."

"How is Beth?" Mardee asked, changing the subject.

Jeff's face brightened, and he said, "She's doing very well. She plays and runs and dances and loves her father."

"She is such an exceptional child," Mardee said. "And so perfectly beautiful."

"Yes," Jeff agreed. "I guess I should be very thankful for this child."

As if on cue, a child's voice trilled through the door. "Daddy, are you there?"

"That's Beth," Jeff said in surprise as he rose and headed for the door.

The door opened before he got there, and Beth ran into her father's arms. "Daddy, we found you," she exclaimed in pleased astonishment.

Mardee looked beyond Beth and saw Heather standing in the doorway. Her perfectly groomed hair and face were complemented by an expensive suit and hat. Her fashionable purse matched her green ensemble. She looks as if she had just stepped off an expensive magazine cover, Mardee thought.

"We parked our car in front, darling," she said in a silky voice. "We know you are walking, so we decided we would give you a ride. We thought you might be here. Are you ready to come home?" Steely eyes ignored Mardee and shot subtle fire at Jeff.

She's snubbing me again, Mardee thought as she felt the anger rising. She deliberately walked forward and stood between Heather and Jeff. "Hello, Heather," she said crisply. "Jeff tells me that Jeanette Reynolds will be visiting you in November."

"Yes," Heather said. "She is a friend from Washington, DC."

"I am going to invite her to speak at a suffrage meeting," Mardee said. "I'm excited at the thought of her being here."

"Yes," Heather said in a condescending voice. "She is here to check into the Indian Affairs Department. She will be very busy while she's here. I don't know whether she will be available."

Jeff spoke from behind Mardee. "We'll do everything we can to help you make connections with Miss Reynolds." He walked toward his wife holding onto his daughter's hand. He held the door for Heather and smiled at Mardee. "It was nice visiting with you, Mardee. I'll talk to you later."

Heather flashed Mardee a look of exasperation as she moved through the door. "Bye, bye," Mardee called in an impersonal voice. She stood in the door and watched the Corbin family walk down the sidewalk. Heather marched stiffly in front of Jeff and Beth. The child skipped along with her father holding tightly to his hand and carrying on an animated conversation. Such a doll, Mardee thought as she watched her antics. Nothing like her mother, thank God.

Mardee went back into her office to gather her things and go. As she drove home, she thought of her visit with Jeff. I guess I should be happy that he's having a rough time, she told herself, but I'm not. I'm sorry for him. And I think the more I see of his wife, the sorrier I am for him. In the two times I've been around her, I perceive her as a woman of bad manners and arrogance. He describes her as materialistic and insincere. Remembering the look she had received as Heather left, she added aloud, "And, she's jealous, too. What a creature!"

Mardee parked her car in the driveway of her home, and happy anticipation at the thoughts of seeing Raquel and Angela and Lola and Robbie pushed everything else away. But one more thought persisted: I must contact Jeanette Reynolds myself and ask her to speak at my rally. Once she's committed, Heather Corbin can't ruin my plans. She instinctively knew an adversary when she met one, and she also knew how to fight one. "You extended the challenge, Heather, and I accept it," she said gleefully as she started toward the house.

13

Mardee sat at her desk contemplating the bright colored fall leaves on the large elm tree outside the window. Maybe Carter will be home for Thanksgiving, she thought. But she knew she didn't dare count on it definitely. The Allies were in control of Europe and armistice agreements were being reached with the countries Germany had invaded and taken over temporarily, and the American soldiers were involved in policing duties. However, the talk was that they would all be returning home in November.

"Well, we kept things going for you, Carter," she remarked as she tidied her desk and took her sweater from the back of her chair. "The clients are coming in steadily now; in fact, I think Will is getting behind. I need to talk to him about getting some part-time help for him."

She picked up the file off the top of her desk and headed for the door. I'll drop by his house and discuss this file as well as the help situation, she told herself.

Mardee knew Will lived on the east side of town in the thick pinion and cedar trees. She crossed a deep arroyo and pulled up in front of a modest adobe house. Will and a woman relaxed in the shaded patio surrounded by multicolored flowers. "I like your roses," she called as she got out of the car and walked on the rock path to the house. Deep rose-red roses splashed vibrant color around the yard.

Will stood to meet his guest with a surprised and flustered look on his face. "Is something wrong, Mardee?" he asked anxiously.

"No," Mardee quickly assured him. "I have a question about the addendum on this contract. The wording seems a little unclear. I want you to look it over and see if we need to make some changes. I thought I would just bring it to you and then get the corrections done before I head home for the day." Mardee handed Will a large manila envelope. "I hate to do this to you at home, but since my time is limited in the office, I thought we should do it now. Sorry for breaking into your evening."

"It's quite all right," Will said, hurriedly. "Why don't you sit here with my wife, and I'll take the papers in the house and reread them. "This is my wife Annie," he added almost as an afterthought.

"Please sit down," Annie said in a soft voice.

Mardee turned her attention to Will's wife and sank down in a soft chair. "This is so beautiful," she said as she swung her arm around in an arc including the sea of flowers behind which the roses formed a striking background. A guitar shaped bird bath nestled among the flowers. Two bluebirds with such a deep indigo color it looked as if they were artificially painted, frolicked and splashed in the cool water. "Such a restful, peaceful place," she said

"Thank you," Annie said with a smile. "I'm glad you like it. We've worked very hard on our landscaping. Will has done most of it."

Mardee continued to study Will's wife. Her dark hair was pulled into a soft coil at the back of her neck. Two beautiful green turquoise combs held it in place. Large dark eyes locked directly into Mardee's gaze. She's a very attractive woman, Mardee realized, but something isn't quite right. Her dark coloring makes her face look very pallid. I hope she's well.

Mardee discarded her thought instantly and said, "I see a woman's hand in all this beauty. I think you must have had a great deal to do with this flower garden, at least with the planning."

Annie smiled apologetically. "Yes, with the planning, but I can't do much of the work. I haven't been very well for several months." She made this statement almost nonchalantly.

"I'm sorry," Mardee said with genuine compassion. "What is the problem?"

"Tuberculosis," Annie answered without hesitation. "Seeing Mardee's reaction, she hastened to reassure her. "I'm doing fine. I get out in the air as much as I can. I think this mountain air is good for me."

Mardee swallowed hard and said, "Yes, that's what they say."

"But, let's talk about you, Mardee," Annie said quickly as if she wanted to put her guest at ease. "I hear you are on your last months of school. You will graduate at Christmas time with a law degree. You must be so proud of yourself. I've never heard of a woman lawyer."

"There are a few," Mardee said, trying to cooperate in Annie's obvious effort to change the subject away from her illness.

"Your husband will be so proud of you when he comes home," Annie continued.

"Yes," he was my inspiration for attempting this almost impossible goal," Mardee said with a slight laugh. "I plan to be a law partner with Carter and Will."

"How wonderful," Annie said with sincere admiration. Mardee suddenly remembered her suffrage meeting coming up the end of October. "I've also been working for women's suffrage. I would like to invite you to our next meeting. Our guess speaker will be Jeanette Reynolds. We will be meeting in the convention room of the La Fonda Hotel."

"I've heard of Jeanette Reynolds," Annie said with animation. "I would love to hear her speak. However, I don't attend public affairs right now. My doctor tells me I must rest and get well." Annie shook her head apologetically.

At that moment, Will came back out of the house to the patio. "You are right, Mardee. That addendum needed some clarification. I have jotted down a couple of explanatory sentences. I'll just take this contract in on Monday and have Raquel make the necessary additions. You don't have to worry about it. You can go on home and check on Lola and the baby."

"Thank you so much," Mardee said with obvious relief. "I would rather go home. I get to take care of the baby tonight while Lola does her performance. I love these times when I'm alone with Robbie. He's such a special little boy. He's so good and so bright and so strong. He's already trying to sit up."

"That is advanced for his age," Annie said.

Will looked preoccupied and said, "There is one thing we should talk about, Mardee. Jeff Corbin approached me this week about doing part-time work for us. I told him we actually need someone right now to help me with my case load."

"I know that, Will. In fact, I meant to talk to you tonight about getting some extra help for you. But, doesn't he have his own practice?" Mardee asked.

"Yes, but he doesn't seem to be very busy right now. If he could do some work for us, it would help him as well as me. We have a case involving an old Spanish Land Claim. He's had a great deal of experience in that type of thing, first working for the legal department in this state, and then doing the same kind of work in Washington, DC."

"I know," Mardee said as her mind pictured his office down the hall from her office when she worked for Governor McDonald. Mardee looked off to the hazy blue Jemez Mountains in the west as she debated the dilemma of Jeff working in the firm. She had been careful to keep a distance between Jeff and herself. But if Will needed help, perhaps she should confront her hesitations about being in close proximity to Jeff. After all, she told herself, he is just an old friend. Why should I worry about him? Carter wouldn't object, I know, as long as he is a good lawyer, and I'm sure he is. Mardee turned her eyes slowly to Will and said, "I will trust your judgment on this one, Will. Let him come in and work a few days, and we'll go from there."

"Thanks Mardee," Will retorted with a big sigh of relief. "I've got too much to do right now, and it shows up in the mistake on this contract. I definitely do need help."

"Very well," she said as she turned to go back to her car. "Nice to have met you, Annie."

"Do come back," Annie called. Mardee turned and waved to the couple standing among their roses. The thought hit her that Will seemed much more confident with his wife by his side and in his home environment. She sent a soft swift prayer, "Please God, let her conquer this illness."

Mardee drove away with mixed feelings about the prospect of Jeff's working in their office. Then her thoughts turned to Will. Poor Will. All he does is work and take care of his sick wife. No wonder he needs help.

When Mardee started down the lane to her house, she let out an involuntary gasp of glee. "Papa's here!" she shouted when she saw his big lumber truck taking up most of the parking area.

Mardee ran in the house and found her father sitting on the living room settee holding Robbie. He was dangling his watch in front of the hypnotized baby. "Careful," he warned as Mardee gave him a big hug. "Don't squeeze the baby too much."

Robbie protested with a grunt and resumed his gaze at the watch.

"Isn't he growing, Papa?" Mardee demanded.

"I'm sure he is," Ben Spencer replied. "Babies have a way of doing that. He's nearly two months old now. He is a big boy for his age."

Robbie shifted his deep blue eyes to Ben as he spoke and gazed at him with baby admiration. Lola came in from the kitchen and said, "I think Little Robbie Blue likes you, Mr. Spencer."

"He would like anyone who had a watch to swing in front of him," Ben declared.

"Put him down in his crib, and we'll eat supper," Lola directed. "I cooked the steak you brought, along with potatoes, gravy, and some green beans."

"I'll hold on to him and feed him some potatoes and gravy," Ben said. "This boy is ready for some real food."

"Papa," Mardee started to remonstrate. "He's pretty young, you know."

"You watch him," Ben said with a smile. "He won't eat it if he doesn't like it."

Ben ate heartily and related all the news from the ranch at the same time. "Floyd is back from France, but he isn't coming home for a while. He did some boxing in the Army, and the former trainer of Jack Dempsey saw him and wants to train him to do some fighting professionally. I don't approve of this, but Floyd is a man. I suppose he can make his own decisions. But I need him at home."

Ben placed a small bite of mashed potato and a bit of gravy on the baby's tongue. Robbie tried to take it in his mouth, but as he worked his tongue back and forth, little of the food stayed in his mouth. "See, he likes it," Ben said with a chuckle.

"What about Charlie and John?" Mardee asked. "How are they doing as young husbands now? That must be an adjustment for them."

"It is, but they're doing fine. I think John would rather farm than work in the sawmill. And Charlie is a little unsettled, too. I don't know what he will do. Roy is young, of course, and he's a better helper to his mother than to me." He tried to feed the baby another bite of food.

"Lola rose from the table and said, "I'll take him and nurse him before I go to the theater. You can feed him when you come back on your next trip." She wiped the potatoes and gravy off the baby's mouth and retired with him to the bedroom.

"What's Mother Spencer doing these days?" Mardee inquired.

"Busy, as always," Ben answered. "That woman never stops. Now she has a Bible Class she teaches for the neighborhood. She's even trying to convert some of the Catholic ladies, but to no avail, I think. What's the news from Carter?"

"I haven't heard from him lately," Mardee said. "I'm hoping the next letter will tell me when he is coming home."

"That will be nice, little girl," Ben said. "I know this hasn't been easy for you."

"I'm almost a lawyer," she said as she passed her father more meat.

"I'm very proud of you," Ben said as quick tears came to his eyes. "You have done what I always wanted to do. I am truly proud of you."

He reached across the table and put his brown gnarled hand over Mardee's small soft one.

Mardee looked closely at her father, and the thought hit her that he was looking older. He's not as young as he used to be, she realized, and she felt the tears sting her eyes. To change the tone of the conversation, she blurted out, "Jeff Corbin is back in Santa Fe. He will be doing some legal work for our firm."

"I'd like to see Jeff," Ben said. The thought of his old friend made him smile. "Maybe I'll look him up before I go back home tomorrow."

"That would be nice," Mardee said in a noncommittal voice as she rose to clear the table. "He has a law office down on San Francisco Street. I'll wash the dishes and you can put your things in my room for tonight. I'll fix a bed on the couch."

"I hate to take your bed, Mardeebird, but I am kinda tired. I can't take these long hours anymore."

Lola gave the baby back to Ben and left for her performance. Ben bounced little Robbie on his knee, and Mardee washed the dishes while her tears added salt to the dishwater. The realization her father was obviously starting to physically fail caused a flood of emotion she could not stifle "No, God, no," she prayerfully whispered. She couldn't imagine life without her father.

As she desperately fought her tears, Mardee suddenly remembered the letter that had been at her office when she went in to work today. Jeanette Reynolds had graciously accepted her invitation to speak at her meeting when she made her trip to Santa Fe. The thought of meeting and talking with this great lady dried her tears. "I will invite her to dinner so I can really visit with her," she murmured. "What an inspiration she will be."

14

Mardee sat in her office the day of her suffrage meeting and let her mind happily dwell on the events she had planned for the celebration. She had contacted Rosa Hidalgo and arranged for her to bring her dancers to her meeting. "This is my last suffrage project," she reasoned. "It will be an extravaganza." She knew she would have a large crowd. The newspaper had run a story about Jeanette Reynolds being the speaker. That would bring the people out. And Mardee hoped her loyal followers would attend, en masse.

I will have Lola sing, she thought. But I won't dance this time. I'll be too busy being the mistress of ceremonies to perform.

Mardee opened the rolled up paper she had picked up when she came to the office. She noted the date at the top, November eleventh, and simultaneously black headlines blasted out at her face. "Germany Signs Armistice." Mardee sat at her desk and devoured the news while tears of joy ran unheeded down her cheeks. "He's coming home. He's coming home." The refrain went on and on in her mind. "Now he's really coming home."

The door opened and Mardee lifted her eyes to two people, a man and a woman entering the room. Through her tears, she recognized Jeff escorting a tall slender young woman. She forgot her tears and said jubilantly, "The war is over. I am so happy."

"Yes Mardee, we all are," Jeff said with a smile. "And I have brought someone to meet you."

Mardee jumped up and said apologetically, "I'm sorry, but I've been

99

sitting here crying like a baby. This means that my husband will soon be home."

The woman stepped forward and extended her hand. "That's quite all right. I understand your tears. I'm sure the country is about to be washed away with them right now. That's good. Perhaps we will all be cleansed of much of the bitterness and sorrow we have endured because of this war. I am Jeanette Reynolds. I wanted to meet you before tonight."

Mardee grasped the congresswoman's hand with both hers and said in an awestricken voice, "I'm so honored to meet you." Then her face clouded with embarrassment, and she pulled back and dashed her hands at her wet tearstained face.

Miss Reynolds opened her purse and drew out her soft handkerchief. "Allow me, my dear," she said as she dabbed gently at the young woman's damp cheeks. Suddenly all Mardee's discomfort vanished, and she said with a radiant smile. "I never quite imagined our meeting would be like this."

"It's perfect," the congresswoman assured her as she carefully folded her handkerchief and put it back in her purse..

Then Jeff took control of the situation and said, "I'm taking you two ladies to dinner. I'll give you five minutes to wash your face and tidy your hair, Mardee. You must look respectable when you dine with Congresswoman Reynolds."

The next few hours were like the answer of a dream to Mardee. The only thing she remembered later about her dinner with Jeanette Reynolds was the lady telling her that she must seriously consider running for elective office. "Our country needs women like you," she had said firmly, and Mardee had known immediately that this had been a subconscious dream of hers ever since she had worked in the governor's office. How astute she is, Mardee thought. I wonder how she knew my innermost thoughts. There must be a mysterious rapport between the two of us.

The entertainment had gone well. Rosa Hidalgo's dancers had performed bombastically as they whirled and stamped through their flamenco dances. Their bright skirts were a mass of color and grace, and their hand movements delicately complemented the stridence of their steps. Lola had sung the New Mexico state song with the passion the occasion demanded. Then she hurried off to the theater for her nightly performance.

Mardee had introduced their speaker of the evening with pride and enthusiasm. Jeanette Reynolds walked onto the stage with modest authority. Her luxurious brown hair was pulled to the top of her head and formed a halo around her interesting face. She was plainly dressed in a white summer skirt and blouse and sensible shoes. Her only touch of fashion was the bright yellow sash which circled her small waist. "This is my tribute to the sunshine of New Mexico," she said with a smile that transformed her plain face as she opened her speech.

Mardee remembered only fragments of the speech, even though the movements and expressions of the speaker held her in rapt attention. Miss Reynolds' large gray eyes were her one claim to beauty, and they seemed to cast a spell over the audience. Her beautifully shaped hands accentuated the air and emphasized her points at appropriate intervals. When she finished her speech, everyone rose as one in a standing ovation. Mardee had never seen a woman wield such a powerful influence over an audience. As she looked back to the moment, it almost seemed like an awesome dream, because Miss Reynolds had raised her head from her bow to the people's tribute and had pointed her hand to Mardee, who sat in the front row. Mardee stood, and the applause had grown even louder, as she joined the congresswoman on the stage. She shared her ovation with me, Mardee marveled in retrospect.

Mardee had arranged a reception for Jeanette Reynolds after the program. Many New Mexico dignitaries were there in honor of the congresswoman. Mardee introduced the governor, the lieutenant governor, and the mayor of Santa Fe. After these introductions, someone rose in the crowd and said she would like to say a few words. As Mardee nodded her permission, she was surprised to recognize Heather Corbin as the speaker. Heather said in a breathy voice, "I am honored to introduce my friend, and the senator from Colorado, Caldwell Johnson. He is visiting briefly in our state." Mr. Johnson stood up to receive his applause. He was a large impressive looking gentleman in a rumpled suit with thinning hair and a genial expression. He waved his hands to the crowd and wiped perspiration from his face before he sat down again beside a beaming Heather.

Mardee had apologized for not recognizing the senator from Colorado and extended her thanks for his attending the meeting. She briefly scolded Jeff to herself for not having told her he would be there.

Gradually, the people had started departing, and Mardee was eventually left alone with Jeanette Reynolds and Jeff. She extended her heartfelt thanks to the congresswoman for speaking at her meeting and told her she hoped to see her again sometime. "When you run for office, I'll come back and campaign for you," Miss Reynolds told her with a twinkle in her expressive eyes.

After Mardee had gotten in her car to drive home, she wondered briefly why Heather had not been there with Jeff and the congresswoman when they went home. "Maybe she was with the honorable Mr. Johnson," she told herself in an amused voice. She could envision the immaculately groomed Mrs. McMahan by the side of the sweaty Senator Johnson. "Quite a pair!" Then Mardee giggled as all the stress of the evening started to evaporate.

Mardee opened her front door expecting to see Addie taking care of the baby, but Lola was already home. "You are late," she said from the kitchen where she was sitting at the table eating a snack. "How did your big shindig go?"

"It went wonderfully," Mardee said happily. "And your song, Lola, was beautiful. You sang like the angel you are."

"Thanks," Lola said, "but I don't know about that angel part."

Mardee waved an admonishing finger in Lola's face just as a knock interrupted their teasing repartee. Mardee ran to the door, immediately feeling anxiety because of this late night visitor. Innately she sensed it could be bad news. She flung open the door to a messenger boy in a red hat. "Telegram," he said as he extended the envelope.

Mardee reached for the yellow piece of paper as her heart started to pound. "Oh dear God," she said and turned from the door without thanking the boy. She was too weak to open the telegram, so she handed it to Lola, who stood behind her, her large eyes conveying the concern she felt. "See what it says," she gasped.

Lola tore open the unwelcome document and her eyes quickly scanned the small paper she withdrew. The tension on her face eased, and she said, "It's from Carter. He says he won't be home for a few weeks. He's recovering in a Paris hospital from receiving a dose of phosgene gas. He says he should be home before Christmas." Lola handed the telegram to Mardee, who read it through carefully before throwing it on the floor and exclaiming, "Those damn Germans! They have gassed my husband." She sank to the floor on rubber legs and pounded the rug in weak protest. "Damn them, damn them, damn them."

Lola dropped on her knees beside her friend and put her arm comfortingly around her shoulders. "But Mardee," she said in a resolute voice "he's not dead. He's in a hospital, and he will get better. It could be so much worse, you know."

Mardee got slowly to her feet with Lola's help and said in a resigned voice, "I think I've always known something would happen. But you're right. He's not dead. He's just burned and having trouble breathing, probably. He could even be blind." Mardee grasped her head in agony as the angry tears flooded down her cheeks. Lola held the devastated young woman until the sobs subsided. Then slowly she lifted her head and said, "But thank God, he's not dead."

15

Mardee attempted to move her uncooperative legs faster down the narrow trench. Her breath came in hurtful gasps, and her arms flailed hopelessly to no avail as she tried to grasp a crooked tree root hanging ominously before her face. She knew she must get out of this trap. She knew she couldn't survive much longer in this putrid air. Her face and eyes burned with fiery fury, and the heat crawled down her throat as she tried to choke lifesaving air into her lungs.

She knew her legs were in slow motion now; they no longer tried to obey her commands of moving faster. She knew she was going to die in this hellhole. She put her hands over her nose to keep out the poisonous fumes as she listened to the desperate whimpers that barely escaped from her tortured throat. "I can't go on," she whispered. "And I can't find Carter."

Hopeless tears ran down Mardee's face as she gave up the fight. She felt suddenly at peace.

"Wake up, Mardee," came a vaguely familiar voice. "Open your eyes, Mardee. You are having a nightmare."

Strong arms enfolded her embattled body, lifting her up higher on her pillow. She barely cracked her eyes open and stared unseeingly into a scene that registered nothing. The only reality was the sobs she heard, and somehow she knew the cries were hers.

"It's all right, dear," the voice continued softly. "You are in your bed, and your bad experience was only a dream. There is no need for tears, Mardee."

Mardee tried to swallow her sobs and opened her eyes wider to ascertain who was talking to her. This time her mind made out the features of Jeff Corbin. She tried to form the words to ask him a question, but her lips wouldn't move. "Carter?" she finally managed to whisper.

"No, Carter is not here yet. But we are sure he will be coming soon."

"I was looking for him," Mardee managed to say.

"You can tell us about your dream later," Jeff said soothingly as he held her hand. "Right now you just relax. Lola will bring you some juice to drink."

Something in the tone of Jeff's voice made her feel at ease, and she lay back on her pillow and sighed with relief, "It was only a dream," she murmured. She rested for a few minutes and then opened her eyes again. She could articulate her words plainly now, although with an effort. "I was looking for Carter in a trench, I think. I couldn't find him, and I guess I was breathing poison gas. I was burning all over, and I knew I was going to die." Mardee paused and then said as the tears started again, "Oh God, is that the way it was for Carter?"

"Here is your juice, dear," Jeff said as he ignored her question. "Sit up and drink your juice."

Mardee obediently did as she was told, and Jeff held the juice to her mouth. She drank a small sip hesitantly and then took a large gulp. The juice tasted good and felt cool in her dry throat. She took the glass from Jeff's hand and said as she regained her sensibilities, "Why are you here?"

"Lola called me," Jeff answered. "She was worried about you. You have slept most of the time for three days. I was going to carry you to my car and take you to the doctor."

"Oh dear God," Mardee said as the hurtful memory of the telegram came back into her consciousness. "I heard Carter has been hurt. I guess I reacted by trying to sleep and never wake up again and face what has happened." Silent sobs shook her small body.

"I think you were just tired. You have been following a pretty stringent schedule, what with your school and your work at the firm and your suffrage extravaganza. Then you got this bad news. I think your body just decided it would withdraw from all the unpleasantness of the real world for a while. How do you feel?"

Mardee's face was expressionless as she replied, "I think I'm fine. I'm strong and healthy. There couldn't possibly be very much wrong with me."

Jeff's face mirrored relief as the worry lines lightened on his brow. "I think you're fine, too. I'm going to have Lola fix you some breakfast. After you eat, you'll feel better. Your body hasn't had any food or drink for three days."

Lola had been standing just inside the bedroom door. She now came forward holding her baby on her hip. "Robbie Blue wants to see you," she said. "He has missed you."

The sight of the little boy was just what Mardee needed to rally her lifeless senses. He reached out his plump arms toward her, and his round face beamed with delight. "How's my boy?" she said as she held the baby close. "I've missed you, too, precious baby."

Jeff headed for the door. "Cook her some breakfast, Lola, and make her eat every bite of it. I must go back to the office and get my work done. We're still very busy, Mardee. That should make you feel better. But, we need you back in the office to help us out. We've missed our girl, Friday. But Raquel has filled in for you nicely."

Mardee smiled over the head of the baby. "I'll be there tomorrow," she promised, and Jeff hurried out the front door.

Later Mardee asked Lola to tell her more of what had happened. She remembered nothing after reading the telegram. "You went to bed and cried the rest of the night," Lola informed her. And you just stayed in bed after that, sleeping and crying. I called DoctorAmble, and he said you were in shock from your bad news. He assured us you would come around, but I got worried this morning after you had been down for three days, and when Jorje delivered milk, I asked him to stop by Jeff's office on his way back to the mercantile and tell him I thought you should be taken to the doctor. I was worried about you."

Mardee shook her head wearily. "I'm sorry I worried you, Lola. And what did you do about singing at the theater?"

"Jet picked up Addie to sit with you and the baby while I was performing," Lola explained. "But she couldn't stay here all the time because of her music students and her boarders. She'll be glad that you are feeling better."

"Well, I've got to feel better," Mardee said resolutely. "I've felt sorry for myself long enough. I'm getting out of this bed and going to class today. I can't miss my classes. I'll never get through with school. Take Robbie Blue so I can get dressed. I'll drink a glass of juice and take some toast to eat on my way to school."

"Are you sure you feel like going back to your regular routine?" Lola asked worriedly. She looked anxiously into Mardee's sunken eyes.

"I'll look better after I splash my face and comb my tangled hair," Mardee said firmly. "I can't miss that business law class today. We've got a test tomorrow."

Mardee's mind went back to other crises in her life. She remembered the lost feeling that had engulfed her as a very young girl after her beloved grandmother had died. The picture of a young girl crying at her grave flashed into her memory's eye after Frankie and Jeff left the ranch.. That was the bare beginning of troubles, she thought, knowing what had happened later Then Jeff had deserted her for Heather and Frankie had been killed in a train robbery. Both of these events had happened fairly close together, and she was sure her world had crumbled beyond repair. But she had rallied with the help of her father and her stepmother. She had recuperated at her home in her beloved mountains and had come back to Santa Fe to face life's challenges again.

The troubled young woman remembered the time she had asked Addie why she always lost everyone she loved. She had felt the cause must lie in some imperfection within herself. But Addie had assured her that was not true. "I'm going to need to talk to her again," she admonished herself. She kept her mind from dwelling on Carter's condition with purposeful determination. "Please, God, not Carter," she prayed ardently. "Not my husband. Not dear, wonderful Carter. I can't make it without him. I can't be alone again."

Mardee knew she was a strong person. She had faced more than her share of tragedies in her twenty-three years, and she had always found a way to keep going toward her goals. "I know You have promised to be with me always," she said as she resumed her conversation with God. "Be with me now, and with Carter. Bring him back to me. Don't take someone else I love. Don't do it again."

Mardee drove up to the college parking area with new resolve and new comfort in her besieged heart.

16

Mardee felt like a zombie as she trod with slow steps to her classes and later made her way up the stairs to her office on wooden legs. She heard nothing else from Carter, and she dreaded each new day and the possible news it could bring.

The only bright spot in her life was the time she spent with Robbie Blue. His deep blue eyes followed her every movement, and he greeted her with a radiant smile when he saw her come home from work. Lola was gone every evening except on Monday nights, and Mardee worked all afternoons and on Saturdays and Sundays. So the full responsibility of the baby fell on Mardee most evenings. But she loved every minute she spent with him, and the sad cloud which hung over her life ceased to exist when she played with him, fed him, changed his diapers, washed his clothes, and hung them out to dry and bleach a pure white in the southwestern sun.

The best part of the day was when she put him in the small tub they used for his bathtub and gave him his nightly bath. He loved the water and kicked and splashed and gasped for breath as his flailing arms threw the water in his eyes and nose. He sometimes surprised himself with his wild antics, but he never cried. "You're my big brave boy," Mardee would say as she took him out at the end of his bath and wrapped him in a soft towel. She would rub sweet smelling baby powder all over his plump body and push his dark hair into ringlets. When she put his soft night clothes on, she would hold him in the rocking chair and give him his bottle. Since Lola was gone so much, she supplemented her mother's milk with milk brought fresh to her every day by Jorje from the mercantile. In the daytime when Mardee went to school or worked, Lola took care of her son. Their schedule worked out well for everybody.

On this evening Mardee had just finished feeding the baby preparatory to putting him to bed, when visitors appeared at her door. Holding the sleepy baby in one arm, she walked briskly to the door. She recognized Will and Annie standing there with big smiles on their faces. Annie was holding a pie from which delicious smells wafted.

"What a nice surprise," Mardee said as she happily greeted her guests.

"I hope you don't mind our dropping by with no warning," Annie said, "but I got ambitious today and baked, and I wanted to bring a pie to you. I know you're so busy you probably don't have time to bake."

"Come on in," Mardee said graciously. "How thoughtful of you. I'll show you my beautiful boy, and then I'll put him to bed."

Annie looked raptly at the baby and said, "What a handsome fellow. He will steal all the ladies' hearts."

"I will chase them all off with a broom," Mardee gleefully retorted. "Set the pie down on the kitchen table while I put this young man down for the night."

Mardee came back from the bedroom to join her friends. "Whew!" she remarked as she wiped her wet brow. "My face is covered with bath water and perspiration." She poured water into a wash basin and splashed it on her face. "Excuse me, folks, but that felt good," she said as she patted her face dry with a towel. "It's a warm evening. Let's go out and sit in the patio."

After everyone was comfortably seated, Mardee directed her eyes to Annie. "I'm so glad to see you," she said seriously. "How are you feeling?"

Annie's quick response assured Mardee her health was improving. Mardee scrutinized her face and noticed the skin was a much healthier tone. Annie's laughing dark eyes added to the perception of improvement in her well-being. "She's so healthy she hurts," Will said, with an attempt toward humor. "She's getting as fat as a pig."

Annie looked at Will with reproachful eyes. "William Cabot," she said in a determined voice. "Do not make statements like that. If I am getting fat, there is a good reason for it."

Will looked embarrassed, and red color crept over his face. "What she is trying to tell you, Mardee, is that she is with child," he said with obvious pleasure.

"Yes," Annie said merrily. "I am going to have a baby. We are so happy. This is what we have wanted for a long time. It's a miracle from God." Annie smiled into her husband's sober gray eyes.

"Your disease?" Mardee asked anxiously.

"All better," Annie said joyously. "The doctor says I'm well on my way to recovery. The clear mountain air and daily exercise did the trick. I wanted to tell you this good news as well as bring you a pie tonight."

"This is the best news I've had in a long time," Mardee said as she embraced the expectant mother. "I'm so happy for both of you." Mardee turned to Will and shook his hand exuberantly. "You'll have a helper we can put to work in the office some day," she said

Will nodded his head and looked pleased. Annie quickly interrupted what he was about to say with a wave of her hands. "She will be a girl who will only help her mother," she stated.

Mardee rushed to Will's rescue. "Girls don't just work at home anymore, Annie. She could work in her father's office. She could even be a lawyer and a partner is his office someday."

"I suppose so," Annie said as she retreated from her decree. "She can be like you, Mardee."

Will and Annie and Mardee settled comfortably into patio chairs, and the conversation drifted from inconsequential subjects to more serious topics. No one spoke of Carter or the war, but those were the foremost subjects on their minds. When the visitors got up to take their leave, Mardee knew from the extra long hugs she received that their thoughts and support were with her. As she waved to them and turned to go back in the house, she thought again of their expected baby. "This is so wonderful," she said aloud. "This baby is a sign to me, Carter. Things are going to work out for us, too."

The heat from the inside of the house hit Mardee in the face as she started in, and she turned around and headed back to the patio and its cool breeze. She sat there looking at the night stars which were bright and thick and appeared close enough to reach up and touch. "God's in His heaven; all's well with the world," she remembered her stepmother saying. Well, it is a better world tonight, she thought, with the war over. And, instead of dread for Carter now, she suddenly felt hope that he would come home soon, and everything would be all right. "Those stars twinkling down at me are trying to bring a message to me from him, I know," she said in a voice husky with emotion. "Those same stars are shining down on him tonight, and they know he is going to be all right."

Mardee sat lost in her thoughts as she contemplated their future after Carter came back home. I will love him and take care of him, she promised herself. I'll make him feel as good as new. He's so strong, nothing will keep him down. She smiled and hugged her legs to her chest. The night air was getting cooler, and her long skirt over her bare legs felt good. She shivered and started to get up, but suddenly she heard soft voices approaching the yard. Mardee sat very still until she made out the figures of Lola and Jet walking toward the house. Why didn't he drive up here? she asked herself.

The couple paused at the gate, and Lola's dark figure nestled in close to Jet's opening arms. Two figures molded together, and the silence told Mardee what they were doing. She felt guilty to be there in such close proximity, but they would see her and be embarrassed if she got up and went in the house, so she just sat very still.

Finally, after a few minutes, she head Lola's low voice murmur, "I wish I could stay with you, Jet. I love you so much."

"I know, darling. I feel the same way. But I promise you we will be together some day in the near future".

"Are you sure, Jet? Do you promise me?" murmured the anxious voice of Lola.

"Give me time to work things out, dear one. We have an exciting life ahead of us. We won't have to stay here too much longer."

There was more silence, and then Lola broke the embrace and came up the walk to the door of the house. Jet turned the other way. Mardee heard him whisper loudly, "I'd better get back to my car. Go in quietly and no one will ever know how late you are getting home. See you tomorrow evening, my pretty."

Lola didn't see Mardee hunched over in the patio chair as she went in the house. She went straight to her room, and Mardee slipped quietly in the house after a few more minutes. Later she lay in bed and thought about this situation. She was totally surprised at this turn of events. She had suspected Jorje had secret feelings for Lola. He came to the house as often as possible and tried to linger longer than necessary to talk to Lola. Mardee could tell that Lola had no feelings for the young man, even though she was nice to him. She always talked to him as if her thoughts were a thousand miles away on someone else. So, it's Jet she's having sweet thoughts about, she now realized. He's the reason her eyes are so luminous these days, and he's why her happy laughter fills the house when she's here. She's in love with Jet Spangler. Mardee took a deep breath and gave a long sigh.

But how is all this going to end? Lola has already proven she lets her heart rule her head when it comes to love. I wonder if Jet is really serious about her? Oh dear, this could all turn out badly. Lola, dear Lola, please use your head, for Robbie's sake if not your own. Mardee rolled over to fall into a troubled sleep. She dreamed of the wind tossing around white hospital beds and brightly lighted stages. She ran through all the turmoil desperately trying to find Carter and Lola. She knew she would never find them.

17

Mardee went into the office on Friday afternoon hoping to get all her work finished so she wouldn't have to come back on Saturday. The work load is getting pretty heavy here, she thought as she put paper in her typewriter. Raquel is working very hard, but it's all we both can do to keep up with it all. Will and Jeff are in the midst of several cases now.

Mardee worked steadily until four o'clock. "I've got to have a break," she said as she looked straight at the carefree picture of Mr. and Mrs. Carter McMahan smiling at her from across the desk. She leaned back in her chair and closed her strained eyes. This is quite an endurance race, she thought. How much longer can I stay in competition, I wonder? Long hours at school, long hours here, and going home to help out with the baby and the chores there. There's certainly truth to the old saying, "Only the strong will survive."

"I wonder how you are doing today," Mardee said as she resumed her conversation with the picture. "Are the burns healing? Is your sight coming back? Have they determined how damaged your lungs are?"

Mardee opened her desk drawer and pulled out the letter she had finally received from Carter. His writing looked familiar even though it was shaky and scribbly. "You never were much of a penman," she said as she again addressed the picture.

Mardee reread the letter. This is probably the twentieth time, she thought, since I got it on Wednesday. It was a short letter which didn't take much time to read:

SOMEWHERE IN FRANCE

My dearest wife,

     I am in a military hospital in France. I was gassed in the Battle of Marne. I got a bad dose, but the doctors seem to think I may come out all right. The pain from the burns is letting up a little. There will be scars, but I never did have a very handsome face anyway, so I shouldn't look much different. My eyes don't seem to be as bad as they thought at first. My sight is improving. They aren't sure how much lung damage there is. I guess I'll know soon enough. Anyway, don't you worry, little sweetheart. I'll get through this and be home to my loving wife soon. I can't wait. I love you always. Your husband, Carter

Mardee folded the letter carefully and returned it to its envelope. Then she pressed it to her lips. He actually wrote this letter himself. His hands touched this envelope. Mardee laid the letter on her desk and put her cheek down on it. It feels so good to touch what he touched, she told herself. It takes away the feeling of utter loneliness.

Mardee's reverie was interrupted by the sound of the door opening. She raised her head to see Jeff entering the room. He hadn't come back to the office since lunch time, and now he wore riding pants and carried a black horse whip in his hand. A broad brimmed hat was cocked jauntily on his head. He was smiling broadly as he stopped in front of her desk. "I have a surprise for you, Mardee," he said as excitement clearly showed in his voice. "Come and look outside."

Mardee had a little trouble shifting out of her thoughts of Carter to understanding what Jeff was wanting her to do. "Come on," he insisted. "I have a surprise for you outside." Mardee rose slowly from her desk, and Jeff grabbed her hand and pulled her toward the door. "See!" he said in an elated voice as he pointed to the curb where two horses were tied. "I'll bet you haven't ridden in months, maybe years. I borrowed these horses, and I'm going to take you riding this afternoon."

"That's a good idea," Mardee said slowly, "but what about the work?"

"It will wait for us," Jeff said glibly. "Besides, we deserve this. You know the old saying, 'All work and no play makes Jack a dull boy.'"

Mardee felt new life stirring inside her. She had been raised on a ranch, riding her little mare, Gypsy, every day. She had been heartbroken to leave her. She had ridden only a few times since coming to Santa Fe.

"These are beautiful horses," she exclaimed. "Where did you get them?"

"From a rancher friend of mine. He brought them in today as a favor for me."

Mardee walked to the black quarter horse and patted his nose. He nuzzled her shoulder and swished his tail smartly from side to side. "What a beauty," she said in a low voice. "He reminds me of my Gypsy."

"Well, run home and change, and get back here so we can head out of the city for the rest of the day." When Mardee hesitated, Jeff pushed her toward her car. "Do as I say. I'll tell Will what we are doing."

Mardee was back in a few minutes, and her pink cheeks and sparkling eyes betrayed her excited anticipation for the coming riding outing. She put one foot in the stirrup, and Jeff easily hoisted her into the saddle. She took the reins and looked down inquiringly at Jeff. "How did you know this is just what I needed?" she asked incredulously.

Jeff got on his mount, a bigger sorrel horse with the lines of a race horse. "Because I know you," he said smugly as he answered her question. "I remember how you love to ride."

"I hope I don't fall off," Mardee said merrily as Jeff kicked his horse and headed him toward the river.

"I'll pick you up," Jeff shouted back over his shoulder.

The two riders followed a path along the Santa Fe River and headed toward the mountains. They were soon in the foothills of cedars and piñions and starting to climb higher in elevation. Jeff took the lead with his big stout horse, and Mardee fell in behind him as her smaller mount picked his way up the mountain side with dainty steps.

Jeff and Mardee stopped to rest their horses when they came to a level meadow where the river meandered more slowly down the mountainside. Jeff rode back to Mardee and asked, "Isn't this a pretty view?"

Mardee surveyed the scene, taking in the golden aspen trees that clustered around the mountain stream like demure ladies dressed for an afternoon tea. Their shimmering leaves fluttered in the breeze as if they were communicating with each other. Mardee giggled at her mental picture and said, "The quaking asps look as if they are having a little chit-chat."

"I love this spot," Jeff said. "I thought you would like it." He turned his horse and started off at a trot. "Can you keep up?" he threw back over his shoulder.

Mardee 's usual response would have been to catch up with Jeff and pass him because of his remark, but instead, she let her horse walk easily behind as her mind went back to the ride she had taken with Jeff when he had left the ranch headed for Santa Fe. She was so young and so in love with him, and she had felt so heartbroken when she watched him disappear into his future. She had begged him to take her with him, and he had promised to help her get to Santa Fe. Well, he kept that promise, she reminded herself. He got me a job with the governor. My expertise with the Spanish language impressed the governor, especially since he didn't speak Spanish. Also, my dad's friendship with him probably helped get the job, too. Anyway, I came to Santa Fe hoping to marry Jeff. But Jeff had another woman on his mind. Mardee abruptly turned her thoughts away from that train of thought. She didn't want to think of Heather today.

I rode up in these mountains once before when Stewart Riley brought me piñion picking, she remembered. She smiled as she thought of the good time they had. Good old Stewart, but it was not meant to be. Now he's happily married to Raquel with a beautiful little girl.

The riders were starting to climb again. Jeff turned around to check on Mardee who was dropping behind. "Come on, slow poke," he yelled.

Mardee waved reassuringly at him and continued on her memory tangent. She was remembering the last time she had ridden a horse. It had been with Frankie, dear Frankie, when he was going to law enforcement school in Santa Fe. She always knew Frankie loved her from the time she was a child, and she had turned to him when Jeff left her for Heather. They had spent Thanksgiving with the Sanchez family and had gone on a ride after dinner. It was a perfect fall ride, only marred with the premonition that their love was not meant to be. Frankie was gone forever by the time she went home for Christmas, killed by a train robber's bullet.

Mardee jerked herself out of her reverie. She couldn't go back to the sad days following Frankie's death. Not now, when so much sadness was festering inside her because of Carter. She dug her spurs into the sides of her horse and pulled up beside Jeff unexpectedly. He turned to her with a smile and said, "Do you think we have ridden far enough? Should we turn back?"

"Yes," Mardee said "I've got to be home in time to take care of the baby when Lola goes to the theater."

The riders turned their horses around and looked back at the scene below them. The city of Santa Fe sprawled out over the foothills. "It looks so small and insignificant from here," Mardee observed, "and it is an important city, the capital of New Mexico."

"True," Jeff agreed, "but small things can be important as well as large things."

Mardee looked at Jeff thoughtfully. "I do appreciate your bringing me on this ride. I love mountains and horses, so if you put the two of them together, nothing makes me happier. This was a break I needed."

"I know," Jeff said as he nodded his head. "And I'll always be here for you when you need me, Mardee. I was not honest with you earlier in our lives, but I'll never let you down again. I really did love you, Mardee, regardless of my actions. Don't ever forget that." His eyes looked deeply into Mardee's. Like turquoise pools of pure water, he thought, but he didn't say it. Instead, he reached over and patted her shoulder. "Now we'd better go. I need to pick Beth up at Addie's house."

"Where is Heather?" Mardee asked without thinking.

"She's away again visiting in Denver. She's helping Caldwell Johnson with some kind of a political affair up there." Jeff looked off into the distance, and his jaw was set in a rigid line.

"Oh," Mardee said quietly. She didn't ask for any further clarification. The expression on Jeff's face told the whole story. "I'm sorry," she said softly.

The lines on Jeff's face relaxed. "It's fine," he said. "Beth and I have a ball together when she's gone." He turned his mount down the mountain, and Mardee followed. Now she had other things to contemplate on the return ride. There may be trouble in paradise, she surmised, and scolded herself because she felt a bit of pleased satisfaction at the thought.

18

Mardee sat at her desk and read the latest letter from Carter with mixed emotions. "I am coming home," he wrote. "That is, I am coming home to America. I will be transferred out of this hospital to the Walter Reed Army Hospital in Washington, DC for further treatment. I am so pleased to be getting closer to you. I will let you know immediately when I arrive at my new destination."

"I must ask Jeff about this hospital," she said aloud as she contemplated this change. "He will know about it since it is located in Washington, DC."

Later when Mardee heard Jeff stirring in his office, she pursued her line of thought and approached him for information on Walter Reed Hospital.

"I have been there," Jeff told her. "It is a large facility, and getting larger. It's been in existence nearly ten years. It started out with about 80 patient beds, but I imagine they are enlarging it now as they take care of their war patients. I'm sure Carter will receive good care there."

"Oh, I wish I could see him," Mardee said longingly. "But Washington, DC is a long distance away."

"Yes, it is," Jeff agreed. "It's about three days by rail,"

Mardee went back to her office and put Carter's letter away. I am thankful he is getting closer to home, she reminded herself and pushed aside her momentary desire to go see him.

November was rushing along. Mardee had less than a month left for her law courses. It was hard to realize she would soon have school out of the way. What a long drag it has been! she thought with a sigh.

Raquel had left a note on Mardee's desk. "Let's make some Thanksgiving plans," she wrote. "Let's have an office Thanksgiving party."

Well, Mardee thought, that's a good idea, but who has room for everybody? There are quite a bunch of us now. She counted: Will and Annie, Jeff and Beth (Heather was still gone), Lola, herself, and Raquel and her family. And I don't have time to cook these days. I'd hate to put the whole dinner responsibility off on Lola. I'll have to think about this.

Mardee closed her door and went on with her office work. Later there was a soft knock, and Will stuck his head in. "I'm going home for lunch," he advised her. "But I was supposed to talk to you about something today."

"About what?" Mardee asked, looking up with interest.

"Annie wanted me to invite everyone in the office to our house for Thanksgiving dinner. How does that sound?"

"Wonderful," Mardee said with enthusiasm. She didn't tell him she had just been wrestling with that subject. "We can all help her with the food," she added. "Lola makes wonderful rolls. She learned from my stepmother. And I used to be a good cook before I got so busy. I'll make pumpkin pies."

"I'll tell Annie," Will said jauntily as he turned to leave. "She'll be so pleased."

"And thanks, Will. Tell Annie we appreciate her so much for doing this for us."

"She's going to enjoy it," Will called back.

The thought of Lola suddenly intruded on Mardee's mind. I know she is getting too involved with Jet Spangler, she thought. Maybe we'll just invite him for Thanksgiving dinner and look their situation over. The conversation she had heard between them recently concerned her. She's obviously crazy about him, but he's older and more experienced, and I don't know what his intentions are. I'll talk to Lola tonight and tell her to invite Jet to our dinner. With that subject decided, Lola went back to her work. "This is a long complicated contract," she groaned.

That night after Lola came home from her performance; Mardee told her of the dinner and proposed the idea of inviting Jet to join them. Lola looked very pleased and said, "That would be so nice, Mardee. Thank you for thinking of him."

"Lola, do you have something to tell me about Jeff?" Mardee pursued.

"What?" Lola asked innocently.

"Like, well, what are your feelings for him Do you like him?"

"I like him very much," Lola said with a radiant smile.

"How much?" Lola asked quickly.

"I love him," Lola said without any hesitation.

Mardee swallowed hard and said, "Does he love you?"

"I think so," Lola answered. "I hope so."

Mardee looked into Lola's face. So beautiful and so naïve, she thought. Aloud, she said, "Be careful, Lola. You don't want to get in trouble."

"Jet would never get me in trouble," Lola protested. "Mardee, you need to really get acquainted with him."

"That's what I plan to do," Mardee said firmly. "I will find out what his plans are for you."

"Don't you trust him?" Lola asked hesitantly.

"I just don't know," Mardee allowed.

A flush of anger crossed Lola's face, and she retorted, "Well, maybe I don't trust Jeff, either. You went riding with him again last week. It seems to me as if you are seeing a lot of a married man."

It was Mardee's turn to react angrily. "Jeff has been kind enough to take me riding to get my mind off my troubles."

"Yes, specifically Carter," Lola came back. "You'd better start wondering what his intentions are toward you. His record isn't the greatest, you know." Lola turned and left the kitchen with a swish of skirts and hair. "I'm going to check on the baby," she said as a conclusion to the conversation.

Mardee sat down at the kitchen table and finished the glass of milk she was drinking. Her anger faded as quickly as it came. She's really right, she told herself. I've enjoyed these rides, but I feel a little guilty about them. Jeff has been a perfect gentleman, but I sense he still cares for me. I mustn't go riding with him anymore.

The next morning was a workday in the office for Mardee. She got there early and opened the mail. She spotted a personal letter for her in the business letters and opened it quickly. It was from Congresswoman Jeanette Reynolds in Washington, DC. It was a short note inviting Mardee to attend the December tenth session of Congress and address this body regarding Women's Suffrage support in New Mexico. "You have sent in an impressive number of names on petitions," Miss Reynolds stated, "and I think it would be well for the congressmen to hear about the strong desire of the women of New Mexico for the right to vote. We are listening to testimony now and will be voting on the issue early next year. Especially, I would urge you to emphasize the Spanish women of the state who have signed your petitions."

"There have been many of them," Mardee said breathlessly.

"I will send you a ticket to travel to Washington, DC by train if you find it in your schedule to make this trip," Miss Reynolds concluded.

Mardee sat very still at her desk looking at the letter. Her mind felt almost in shock. A trip to Washington, DC, she thought over and over. It just didn't seem to register. But thoughts started racing through her head. I am out of school at that time. But I don't think I'd have the nerve to travel that far by myself.

Her first impulse was to talk to Jeff, and she ran into his office and threw the letter on his desk. "Read it," she ordered.

Jeff looked up at Mardee in mild surprise and scanned the letter. Then a broad smile spread over his face. "You are invited to speak to the Congress of the United States. This is unbelievable!"

"What's so unbelievable about it?" Mardee asked defensively. "I could speak to them."

"Of course you could," Jeff said with a laugh. "But they just don't usually invite women to address them."

"I'm afraid I couldn't make that long trip by myself," Mardee said honestly.

"Of course you could," Jeff said reassuringly. He was silent a moment and then added, "I have an idea. Why don't you ask Jeanette if you could bring Lola? If a Spanish woman spoke to them in person, that would be more effective than your telling about this group of women. Lola would make a very good impression, and with her stage training, she would not be intimidated by the honorable members of Congress."

Mardee's face mirrored excitement at this prospect, and she said, "Do you really think she might be interested in Lola?"

"Sure, and after all, she helped you with those signatures. She interpreted for you and performed for you."

Mardee turned quickly and said, "I'm writing a letter of acceptance right now, and I'll ask Miss Reynolds if Lola can come."

Jeff shook his head and said, "Washington, DC will never be the same after you two women invade it." But Mardee didn't hear him; her mind was on her letter and the trip.

All coolness between the girls was forgotten when Mardee told Lola of the plan that night. Lola was equally as excited about the prospects of this trip as Mardee. "Sybil can take my place in my roll at the theater," she planned aloud. "She's been dying to take over for me. I'm sure Jet will let me go."

"And we can leave the baby with Addie," Mardee said, joining in the planning. "I'm sure she will do that for us."

The two young women joined hands and danced joyously around the kitchen. "Over the hills and over the dell, to the Congress we will go," Mardee sang repetitively until both girls sat down to catch their breath. "Wait a minute," she cautioned. "We have to hear from Miss Reynolds before we know for sure we are going. We'd better not start counting our chickens before they hatch, as Mother Spencer used to say."

Lola's luminous eyes shone, and she said with certainty, "I know we're going, Mardee. I feel it in my bones, as my father used to say. We're going on a long trip."

"A long, long, trip," Mardee corrected her. "We'll probably sleep on the train two nights before we get there."

The young women from the Manzano Mountains of New Mexico went to bed that night in an aura of anticipation and excitement at what could happen to them. Mardee was too nervous to sleep, and as she lay pondering the trip, the thought suddenly came to her head like a bolt of lightning: Carter may be there in the hospital by that time. I'll ask Miss Reynolds if she can arrange for me to visit him while I'm there. "Thank you, Lord," she said aloud. "What was that scripture? 'All things work together for good for those that love the Lord.' That's it, and dear God, I do love you and thank you." She turned over and drifted into a peaceful and hopeful sleep.

19

Thanksgiving at the Cabots was a gala affair. The smell of the roasting turkey permeated the air as guests arrived in high spirits, bringing their various culinary offerings. Lola had baked rolls, Mardee brought pumpkin pies, Raquel brought fresh tortillas and homemade raspberry jam, and her parents brought chokecherry wine. As Miguel passed out the drinks in Annie's crystal glasses, he proclaimed, "The nectar of the chokecherry trees of La Cienaga, made by the hands of the loveliest lady in La Cienaga, Teresa Sanchez. Drink and enjoy!"

"To our host and hostess, Will and Annie," Jeff toasted with raised glass.

"To Miguel and Teresa, the winemakers," Will said as he raised his glass.

"To Thanksgiving, our country, and our men who fought for our country," Mardee toasted. "Especially to Lieutenant Carter McMahan." She didn't add, and to our anniversary, which is in a few days. The anniversary of our first year of marriage.

"To our children, Angela, Beth, Robbie, and the new baby to come," Annie said softly.

"To all of us gathered here on this Thanksgiving Day, 1918. May we always be together in hearts, if not in person." This was Lola's toast, and everyone drank heartily.

After she sipped her drink, Mardee looked keenly at Lola. Her eyes were on Jet, and Mardee was momentarily troubled by the true meaning of Lola's words. Is there a secret message being transmitted between those two? she wondered. But there was no time for further speculation as the women continued the food preparation in the kitchen and the men started domino games on the patio. Angela and Beth ran excitedly around the yard in the late fall sunshine playing their imaginary games.

"Don't fall in the birdbath," Jeff counseled Beth.

"Don't get your pretty dress dirty," Raquel counseled Angela.

The ladies were making progress with the food, and Mardee suddenly felt the need to escape from the hot kitchen to get some air. She walked down a path that led to the woods behind the house. The thick dark green piñons grew in abundance here, and she took deep grateful breaths of the pungent air. "It's almost as good as the pine scented air of the Manzanos," she remarked to a squirrel sitting placidly on the branch of an unusually tall piñion tree.

The thought of home suddenly stabbed at her heart, and she felt the quick tears fill her eyes. We're all scattered, it occurred to her. Floyd is somewhere learning to be a boxer; Charlie and John are married, and Papa and Mother Spencer and Roy are alone today. She knew she couldn't allow herself to continue in this vein of thought, so she impatiently wiped the tears away and scolded herself. That's the way of life, you know. It goes on, and it changes, she admonished herself.

Mardee walked around a turn in the path and came unexpectedly upon another hiker. Jeff stood with his back to her, looking down at the view of the city of Santa Fe. "Oh, I'm sorry," Mardee said. "I didn't mean to intrude."

Jeff turned and looked at Mardee. His face was thoughtful, and his eyes were soft and introspective. "That's all right, Mardee. Robbie was getting fussy, so I rescued him from his pallet on the patio and brought him for a walk." Jeff looked fondly down at the sleeping infant he held in his arms. "See, the fresh air put him to sleep. Please join us. I was just enjoying the solitude. I have a great deal to think about these days."

"Maybe I should be on my way," Mardee said as she started to walk on.

Jeff put out his hand and said, "Please stay and talk with me for a little while. We seldom get a chance to be alone. I would like to talk with you. Please."

The intensity in Jeff's voice alerted Mardee to the seriousness of his state of mind. She stood still and looked into his face. "What is it, Jeff?"

Jeff put his head down and said nothing for a long moment. When he raised it, Mardee could see the pain in his eyes. "It's about Heather," he said haltingly. "She's left me, Mardee. She wants a divorce. She wants to marry her political friend."

"Caldwell Johnson?" Mardee asked is disbelief. "She wants to marry him? Why?"

"Because he's rich and can give her the material things I can't," Jeff said sadly.

"What kind of a reason is that?" Mardee asked with disdain. "I wouldn't marry him if he had all the money in the world."

"But you are different, Mardee. Heather thinks only of herself and what she wants. I don't think she is capable of truly loving anyone."

"What about Beth?" Mardee asked. She was beginning to comprehend the seriousness of this matter.

"She won't get her," Jeff said in a steely voice. "She left her, and she can't have her. The law is on my side there."

Mardee looked at the hurt expression in Jeff's eyes. "I'm so sorry," she said.

Jeff turned to Mardee and put his hand on her shoulders. "Dear little Mardee," he said as he looked poignantly into her eyes. "After what I did to you. I'm the one who is sorry, Mardee. I made a big mistake. Now I'm paying for it." Jeff turned away with a hopeless sigh.

Mardee walked around to face Jeff again. "But you've got Beth," she said intensely. "You've got the dearest little girl in the world. Maybe it wasn't such a bad mistake after all."

"You're right, Mardee. You're always right. And I love you, Mardee. I always have and I always will."

"Jeff," Mardee said as she involuntarily held up her hand as if to curb his words. "Please."

"Don't panic, Mardee. I won't say it again, but I had to tell you this once. I love you for so many reasons: for your kindness, your beauty, your intelligence, your integrity, your courage. You are a one of a kind, Mardee, and Carter is a lucky man to have you for his own."

Mardee stood as if transfixed while she gazed into the face of the man she had loved so long ago. He did love me, she thought. But it is too late now. "We should go," she said in a voice that sounded strangely calm. "Annie will have the dinner ready by now."

"Yes," Jeff said with a husky catch in his voice. "I'd better get this baby back before his mother thinks he has been kidnapped."

Mardee and Jeff walked back in the Cabot home just as the group was getting ready to sit down for the meal. Jeff put the baby in the new crib awaiting Annie's new arrival. Mardee stood beside him and made note of his tender expression as he smiled down at the sleeping infant. So sad, she thought. He wanted a son so badly.

Will said a brief prayer, and everyone heaped their plates with the bounteous meal. Mardee ate like a zombie and tasted nothing. I know this food is good, she thought inanely, but the only thing real to me is that Jeff loves me. Jeff has always loved me, yet he married another woman. I don't understand all this.

Mardee's thoughts were suddenly interrupted by someone directing a question to her. "Have you heard from Jeanette Reynolds?"

Mardee put her napkin to her mouth in order to gain a moment to think, and then said, "Oh yes, I did hear from her. She extended an invitation to Lola and me to be her guests in Washington, DC so we can address Congress regarding a proposed bill for women's voting rights. She will send us tickets to travel there by train."

There were remarks of awe and admiration from the group and good wishes extended to them for their safe travel. Mardee watched Jet's face and pointedly asked him "What do you think of this, Jet? Are you going to be able to do without Lola for a few days?"

"It will be difficult, but we will manage," Jet said glibly. "Sybil, Lola's understudy, will take over for her. She'll do fine."

Lola looked adoringly at Jet and said, "I will miss everyone so much."

"But you will enjoy Washington, DC," Mardee said a bit too forcefully.

"Oh yes," Lola said and apologetically nodded her head.

The topic of conversation changed and eventually Mardee's dessert was served. "You haven't lost your touch," Jeff said after he took his first bite. "I remember eating your pumpkin pie at the ranch."

At the ranch, a lifetime ago, Mardee thought sadly. Before the unwelcome tears came again, she hastily said, "Stewart, do you remember your first Thanksgiving in New Mexico at the Sanchez Ranch before you married Raquel?"

"Oh yes," Stewart said with a grin on his ruddy face. "That's the first time I ever tasted red chili. I thought I would die. I really thought I would choke to death."

"I saved him with water and tortillas," Teresa said with a smile. "Now he eats my red chili with no problems."

Everyone laughed, and the festive tone of the day was back. Mardee avoided Jeff's eyes as she made light conversation with everyone but him.

Later that night Mardee lay in her bed and reviewed the day's revelations from Jeff. I guess I've known this feeling Jeff has for me existed ever since he's been back, but I wouldn't acknowledge it. Now I have to: I have no choice. He's going to be single, but that can't change my commitment to Carter. Lord, help me to be strong in the coming days. I've got a lot to face, and I can't do it without You. Mardee stared into the dark. "Life is such a battle," she said aloud. "The fight is never over. Sometimes I get so tired."

20

Mardee and Lola dropped the baby off at Addie's house and turned the car southward toward Albuquerque. "We're going shopping," Mardee said as if she couldn't believe her own words. "We're going to buy new clothes in the big city so we will look glamorous when we get to our nation's capitol. We mustn't look like country bumpkins."

"But that's what I am," Lola said hopelessly. "I'm really just a half Mexican girl from the mountains. We might as well face it. It's different with you." Lola put her head back on the seat and looked miserable. "You're educated and smart. I'm just dumb and stupid."

"None of that," Mardee said sharply. "You are the reigning drama queen of Santa Fe. You have a golden voice, plus beauty, grace, and charm. You are the toast of New Mexico. That is the way I will introduce you in the United States Congress." Mardee looked swiftly to her right to see the effect of her words, and then added. "I mean it, Lola. Sit up and be proud of yourself."

Lola straightened up and said, "I am proud of myself, especially when I look back a year and see what has happened to me since I came here. But I never quite forget where I came from, and that I have a baby, and I'm not married. Who will ever love me enough to forgive me my shame? Certainly no one will ever want to marry me."

Mardee knew a good answer to this question was important. She sent a quick, "Help me, Lord," prayer through the open window, and slowly answered, "Lola, a good man who loves you sincerely will not hold your past against you. He will have faith in what you are now and forgive you your mistakes. We all have lived imperfect lives, Lola, including me. I have tried to tell Carter about my past loves, but he doesn't care, and he won't even listen. He just loves me for the way I am now. He understands my heart, and he knows I would never be untrue to him. You'll find that kind of a man someday."

"I hope you're right," Lola said with a sigh.

"What about Jet?" Mardee couldn't help asking. "I think I know how you feel about him. How does he feel about you?"

"He likes me," Lola said with a faint smile. "But I don't think he will marry me."

"It's a little soon to think of marriage with him, anyway. You haven't known him that long.," Mardee reasoned.

"He's thinking of my career," Lola said. "He thinks I could be a big star."

"And he may be right," Mardee said. "But let's think of what we are going to buy today. I think I will look for three outfits. I need a new suit to wear when I appear before Congress. I need a new dress to wear when I visit Carter, and I need an evening outfit in case we get to go to the theater. Miss Reynolds said she would try to get us tickets to the Booth Theater. Doesn't that sound exciting?"

"It would be nice to sit in the audience for a change and watch a show instead of being on the stage doing the show," Lola agreed.

"You know, I was reading an article in a magazine recently that described the new styles. Shorter skirts are in fashion, even up to the knee. Can you imagine?" Mardee giggled and cast a provocative look in Lola's direction.

"Well, we've got the legs for those skirts," Lola said daringly as she joined in Mardee's mood.

Later Mardee parked her little Ford car on Central Avenue, and the girls proceeded to take in the sights and stores of Albuquerque. They walked slowly down the sidewalk, gazing in the store windows with round eyes. "I didn't know so many clothes existed in the world," Mardee said as she stared in awe at a thin mannequin wearing a claret red dress of silk organza with a myriad of sheer ruffles around the neck, on the sleeves, and around the skirt.

"I don't like that dress," Lola said. "It's shorter in the front than in the back."

"That's the style," Mardee explained patiently. "It's supposed to look chic that way."

"It just looks lopsided to me," Lola disagreed.

"That goes along with the 'flapper' concept," Mardee explained further. "The modern styles exemplify the new freedom women are feeling now. The loose waists and lack of the necessity of wearing a corset go along with this theory, also."

"Thank goodness for the elimination of the corset," Lola said with relief.

"Let's go in here," Mardee said excitedly. Then she lowered her voice and whispered, "I've heard there is a new underwear garment which is one piece, and you step into it. We must check that out."

The next few hours went fast as the girls looked and modeled and wrestled with fashion decisions. The clerks, sensing these shoppers would make serious purchases, bustled around the aisles of their stores, desperately trying to find just the right clothes that could not be resisted. By early afternoon, each girl had purchased a stylish suit, a long evening dress, and a short formal dress. Mardee had outfits in colors of ashes of rose, seawood, and falcon grey. Lola had chosen clothes in shades of garnet red, cocoa brown, and lapis blue. Each girl had purchased a pale pink one-piece, step-in underwear set, and a pair of sheer silk hose. Mardee bought a wide brimmed shamrock green hat with a sweeping feather curling around her face to wear with her grey suit. Lola felt she didn't have the money to buy a hat. She reasoned that she could borrow one from the theater costume department if she wanted one, anyway.

"We have green shoes that would match your suit perfectly," she told Mardee.

The satisfied shoppers made their way back to the car and loaded down the back seat with their purchases. "Now we know how it feels to be rich and buy beautiful clothes," Mardee said with satisfaction as she got in the car.

"Yes, but we're rich only for a day," Lola pointed out.

"I'm starved," Mardee said as she drove the car down Central Avenue. "Let's go to the Harvey House to eat."

The Harvey House was the dining restaurant for travelers getting off the trains that stopped in Albuquerque. It was located next to the depot. Mardee easily found a parking spot and the two young women walked into the big dining room.

"Isn't this elegant?" Mardee whispered to Lola as they were escorted to a table by a fresh-faced young woman in a starched uniform. They sat down and tried to appear nonchalant as they perused the large menu which was put in front of them.

"I want a ham sandwich and a piece of lemon pie," Mardee said as she closed the menu and looked around with interest.

"Maybe I just want a bowl of soup," Lola said uncertainly.

"Get what you want," Mardee instructed. "I'm paying for this. How about some peach pie with your soup?"

"That would be nice," Lola said with relief. Mardee had correctly guessed she had been mentally counting the money in her purse and had decided she had no choice but to eat a scant lunch. She knew she would love to have some pie. "I hope they make it like Mother Spencer makes hers," she remarked hopefully.

"Did you know that Mother Spencer worked here when she came west?" Mardee asked Lola.

"No," Lola said.

"Well, she did. She came through Albuquerque on the train on her way to California to teach school. She had come from Kansas, and she was short of money, so she decided to stop off here and work for a while before she went on the California. She got a job here in the Harvey House."

134

"It's hard to imagine her here," Lola said as she looked around at the perfectly groomed waitresses scurrying from table to table.

"I can imagine her here," Mardee stated "She would fit perfectly here with all this work and cleanliness. You know, they won't hire just anyone. You must be a well-mannered, nice looking, intelligent young woman of high morals to work here."

"On second thought, I guess she would fit here," Lola said. "She certainly measures up to those standards."

"Yes, she's quite a lady," Mardee said as she thought fondly of her stepmother. "Anyway," she went on, "my father came here to eat and saw her and knew immediately he wanted to take her back to the mountains with him. He gave her a job teaching the sawmill school, and took her home with him. Two years later they were married."

The young women enjoyed their food and talked animatedly of their trip to come, but they couldn't linger long. Lola had to be back in Santa Fe for her evening performance. They sped back up the hills and Mardee took Lola straight to the theater just in time to change into her stage costume.

Lola walked in the theater door swiftly, not noticing that Mardee was following her. I think it is time Jet and I had a visit, she thought as she headed for Jet's office. She knocked gently and opened the door. Jet glanced up with a startled look from a script he was reading. "You got back all right, I see," he stated cryptically.

"Oh yes," Mardee said brightly. "We found some beautiful clothes, but we knew we couldn't stay too long. The show must go on, you know."

"Yes," Jet said dryly. Mardee could see her humor wasn't appreciated.

"Do you have time to talk with me a few minutes?" Mardee asked, changing to a serous demeanor.

Jet looked at his watch. "I have a few minutes," he said, emphasizing the word, 'few.'

"Good," Mardee said decisively. "I'll come right to the point. You mentioned once that you had show business contacts who would be looking Lola over. Did that ever happen?"

Jet returned Mardee's gaze with inscrutable eyes. "As a matter of fact, it did."

"What did they think of her?" Mardee demanded.

"They liked her, but she's young and inexperienced and needs lots of direction in the show business world. I think that all goes without saying."

"She does have talent, though," Mardee declared emphatically.

"Of course, she has talent. She's the lead in my show, isn't she?"

Mardee didn't like the way Jet looked at her or the tone of his voice. "I want you to know, Jet, that even though Lola is young, she has people watching over her who will not let her be taken advantage of. I expect you to be open and honest with her and work for her best interests." Mardee looked Jet straight in the eye and the tone of her voice emphasized the seriousness of this matter in her mind.

Jet stood up, signifying this conversation was about to end. "I appreciate your interest in Lola," he said in icy tones. "I must check on my performers. The curtain goes up in a few minutes. I'll see you to the door."

Mardee found herself being propelled out Jet's office door by a firm hand on her elbow and headed toward the entrance. Jet bowed slightly and turned and left her at the door.

"Well!" Mardee said in exasperation. "I don't think he wants to talk to me." She hadn't really learned anything from this encounter with Jet about his feelings for Lola, but her innate premonitions of distrust for this man and his intentions still persisted, even stronger now. However, she didn't have time to dwell on this problem. It was time to go pick up Robbie Blue. At the thought of his sweet face, her frown of frustration and aggravation melted away. She looked forward to a long evening alone with her favorite little ray of sunshine.

21

Another boy in a red hat; another telegram. Mardee's face paled as she reached for the envelope. No one was there to read the message for her this time, so she steeled herself to read the contents. "Please, God," she whispered, "Let him be all right."

With an effort, she focused her eyes on the slip of paper. It read, "arrived at walter reed hospital today stop will be here for indefinite period stop love stop carter stop"

Mardee collapsed at her desk and put her head down on the telegram. He's getting closer to home, she told herself. Someday he'll be back here to me. Someday I will see him.

"Someday, my foot!" Mardee shouted as she jumped to her feet. ""He's in Washington, DC. I can see him when I go there next week." She pulled a piece of paper out of her desk drawer and hastily scrawled a brief message on it. "Dear Miss Reynolds," she wrote. "My husband, Lieutenant Carter McMahan, is now in the Walter Reed Hospital recovering from being gassed in France. Could you please arrange for me to visit him when I am there? There isn't time for you to let me know, but I'll be hoping I will be able to see my husband very soon after I arrive in Washington, DC." She signed the letter, "Affectionately, Mardee McMahan."

Mardee put the note in a stamped envelope and hastily ran to the post office to mail it. After posting the letter, she stood for a moment concentrating on her busy schedule. I'll go back to the office and finish my work there. Then I'll go to the library to get some research done so I can finish my last report that is due by Monday. Then I have finals to take next week, and school is over with. I can't really believe I am about finished. What a long hard drag this has been.

Mardee walked slowly back to the office enjoying the bright winter sun. Where has this year gone? she wondered. Last week was the first anniversary of our wedding, and Carter wasn't here. This is not the way a normal marriage should be, but I don't think I've ever had a normal life. Things happen differently for me than for other people.

Mardee's thoughts went to Jeff and the complications his presence had created in her life. He stayed in his office most of the time and worked with his door closed, but she felt she knew every breath he took. When she caught occasional glimpses of his face, her heart pounded compassionately as his countenance plainly mirrored the pain he was suffering because of the break-up of his marriage. The gray was very apparent in his hair now, and his mustache was almost white. The only time he looked happy was when she saw him with Beth. As this little sprite skipped along beside him, the lines on his face lessoned, and the smile in his eyes was back.

Mardee pulled her thoughts away from Jeff and back to her husband. The idea of actually seeing him again so soon took her breath away. What an exciting trip this is turning out to be, she told herself gleefully.

Time rushed by swiftly as Mardee attended her last classes and packed her suitcases for her trip. Jeff had offered to take Lola and her to catch the train in Lamy, so as they rode the twenty miles over the mountain to the station, Mardee felt as if she were riding on a dream cloud to paradise. It wasn't until Jeff was given hurried thanks, and they were settled in their seats that Mardee gave a big sigh and said, "I'm really on this train. I'm really going to Washington, DC and to Carter. Tell me we're on our way, Lola."

"We're going, I promise you," Lola said with a radiant smile. Look at the black smoke rolling past our window. We're climbing a mountain heading east."

The excited chatter of the young women died down as the train traveled on and on over the mountains and valleys of New Mexico and

Colorado and into the flatlands of the Midwest. "We can't go to bed until we change trains in Kansas," Mardee told Lola. "After we get on our next train, then we can settle down for the night."

"It will be exciting sleeping on a train," Lola said.

"It should rock us to sleep," Mardee said.

Lola had fixed lunches for them to eat on their first traveling day. They had fried chicken and doughnuts and apples. The porter brought them cartons of milk for ten cents, and they feasted royally as they watched the unfamiliar scenery rush by their window.

"I would never want to live in this flat country," Lola remarked.

"Nor I," Mardee said in agreement. "I must always have my mountains."

The young women sleepily changed trains in Wichita, Kansas. The porter led them to their sleeping quarters. "I will sleep in the upper bunk," Mardee offered. "I wouldn't want you to fall off."

"Thank you," Lola said gratefully. She was already becoming a little stressed out from this adventure.

Mardee said a prayer and fell asleep instantly. The past weeks had been hectic, and her body was ready for rest. The train carried them north and east, and by morning they were going through the train yards in Chicago. The porter awakened them and they went to the dining car to eat breakfast.

"Don't stare at the waiter," Mardee whispered to Lola.

"But, his face is so dark," Lola whispered back.

"I think I'll have hotcakes," Mardee said loudly. "I'm suddenly hungry."

"Just order me the same," Lola said as she shrank back from the waiter and looked nervously out the window.

After their order was taken, Mardee said softly to Lola, "We are probably going to be seeing many different kinds of people that we are not accustomed to being around. We must act nonchalant about it. We don't want people to think we are ignorant hillbillies."

"Maybe that's what I am," Lola said petulantly.

"No," Mardee said patiently, "You are the beautiful and talented drama queen of Santa Fe. Remember?"

Lola relaxed and smiled. "I'll try," she said.

After breakfast, the girls settled down for another long day's travel as they went due east. "We're heading for New York City," Mardee said with satisfaction. "When we get there, we will have less than a day's travel left."

Lola propped her pillow under her head and closed her eyes. "I'm going to sleep until we get there," she proclaimed.

"You'll have to wake up to change in New York City," Mardee told her.

The train moved unendingly down the silver tracks, stopping briefly at towns along the way. Passengers got on and passengers got off. This is never ending, Mardee told herself as she dug out a book to read. "What a big country we live in," she said aloud.

"I prefer Santa Fe," Lola said from the depths of her pillow.

"Are you getting homesick already?" Mardee asked impatiently. "You're getting crabby."

"I'm sorry," Lola said sincerely. "I do miss Robbie Blue."

"Anyone else?" Mardee asked. "How about Jet?"

"Yes," Lola said in a small voice.

"You'll have all of Washington, DC at your feet, Lolita. Forget about Jet."

Lola answered the command with a noncommittal grunt. Mardee opened her book and pursued the misadventures of the heroine in "The Perils of Pauline."

A wait and a change in New York City, and one more night on the train brought Mardee and Lola into the train depot in Washington, DC on a Thursday morning about ten o'clock. After the conductor had helped the two women down the steps, a black uniformed man approached and asked respectfully, "Mrs. McMahan and Miss Tompkins?"

"Yes," Mardee said eagerly. "She's Lola Tompkins, and I am Mardee McMahan."

The man gathered up the luggage and said, "I am Rupert, Miss Reynold's driver. Please follow me. I will take you to your hotel."

Mardee and Lola followed the driver with quick steps. He led them to a black limousine and set the suitcases down at the back of the vehicle. He opened the door and Lola jumped agilely into the black leather interior. She sank down in the soft seat and automatically rubbed her hand over the smooth texture. Mardee followed suit and both women exchanged satisfied smiles at the circumstances in which they now found themselves. Rupert loaded up their suitcases in the trunk of the car and shut the door with a resounding bang. He came around to the driver's side and slid easily into the seat. The motor of the car had been left running, and he pressed the gas feed pedal and pushed the gear shift, and they moved slowly away from the train station. Mardee closed her eyes and said exuberantly, "We're here! We're actually here in the capital of our nation. Two women from the mountains of New Mexico. We're really here!"

Mardee glanced at Lola. Her eyes were two big dark pools of seething excitement. She feels the way I do, Mardee realized. Oh Papa! If you could see me now!

"I am taking you to the Shamrock Hotel," the driver said in stilted English. "It is a small, rather nice hotel. You will enjoy it there."

Rupert must be English, Mardee thought. I must try to have some private conversation with him. I'll bet he has some interesting stories to tell. Aloud, she said, "This is going to be such a wonderful visit. Look, Lola, there is the dome of the capitol in the distance."

"Your hotel is in walking distance of the capitol," Rupert informed them.

"We will walk around to all the sights," Mardee said. "We must see everything while we are here."

"Miss Reynolds told me to tell you to have lunch at your hotel today and relax this afternoon. The Congress is in session, so she can't join you until this evening when we will pick you up and take you to the theater. We will come for you at seven o'clock. You may wear evening clothes, please."

"Certainly," Mardee said and gave Lola an all-knowing look which reminded Lola she had insisted they buy evening apparel..

The driver pulled up to the front of their hotel under an impressive awning. While he held their car door open, the doorman opened the big hotel door wide. "Welcome to the Shamrock, ladies," he said graciously.

Mardee and Lola stepped into the lobby of their hotel, their heads held high and their steps firm and dainty. The glance they exchanged with each other plainly said, "We are fine ladies and will be treated thusly." A bellhop jumped to attention and came to take their luggage. The driver walked with them over to the registration desk and gave the information needed to claim their rooms.

While the paper work was being done on their registration, Mardee looked around the large lobby. It had beautiful high ceilings with huge crystal chandeliers elegantly guarding the luxurious interior. The furniture was large and made of heavy dark wood. The chairs and divans were covered with dark green velvet upholstery. Even the large gold spittoons looked elegant as they rested on the lush green carpet.

"We'd better have a few drops of Irish blood flowing through our veins or we might get kicked out of here," Mardee whispered.

"I think my father does have Irish blood in him," Lola said seriously.

"Papa does, too, so we're fine," Mardee assured her.

The bellhop took the women to their room and set their luggage down. "Is there anything I can get for you?" he asked courteously.

"No, we're fine," Mardee said, and as he kept standing there, she suddenly realized he was waiting for a tip. She hastily dug through her purse and came up with a fifty cent coin. "Here you go," she said grandly as she dropped it into the outstretched hand.

"Thank you," the bellhop said in an expressionless voice. He turned and left hurriedly.

"Why did you give him money?" Lola asked in a baffled voice.

"It is customary," Mardee said easily. Actually, she had never tipped anyone before, but she had heard people talk about this custom when they traveled to large cities. "Let's unpack now," she said happily. "Then we'll go downstairs and find the restaurant. I'm starved. This is an Irish hotel; maybe the food is Irish, too. Maybe we can eat a sour kraut and corned beef sandwich."

When Mardee and Lola sat down in a small white booth decorated with green shamrocks, a pert waitress approached them and asked, "What can I bring you to drink? Our specialty is our Irish coffee." Mardee smiled and said, "Not this early in the day. I would like a glass of lemonade, please, and a menu."

Lola ordered lemonade also, and they studied the menu given to them by the waitress. The food on the train had ceased to taste good to them, and they were very hungry. They decided on the corned beef sandwich with a bowl of potato soup. They also got tempted by the apple pie, so they ordered one piece to split between the two of them. They ate their first meal in Washington, DC with gusto and unabashed pleasure.

Suddenly the small dining room was filled with fiddle music as an old man entered the room playing an Irish song with a fast tempo. An older lady at a booth near them jumped up and started dancing a jig to the song. Her feet moved in quick intricate steps in time to the music, but her arms and hands remained still at her sides.

"That's a little different step than our southwestern dances," Mardee noted.

"I prefer to dance with a partner," Lola remarked.

"Well, anyway, we've got music and dancing with our meal. We can't complain."

Others joined in the dance, and it seemed to be considered perfectly correct to eat a while and then dance a while. The fiddler kept playing, and the people kept dancing. When he started playing the poignant waltz,

"River Shannon," the dancers sat down and listened and ate with a sad, dreamy look on their faces. "They still have a very deep feeling for their homeland," Mardee informed Lola.

A couple at a table close to Mardee and Lola were carrying on a vibrant conversation in another language. They had the coloring of an American, but their gestures were more dramatic, and their voices were raised often in animated inflections. "What language are they speaking?" Lola asked.

"I don't know," Mardee said. "Perhaps it is Italian. I hear some words that sound similar to Spanish. Anyway, there seem to be a lot of foreigners here. We are used to three cultures in our state, Anglo, Spanish, and Indian. There are more than three nationalities of people here, I think. Americans are almost in the minority in this hotel. I suppose people come from all over the world to visit our beautiful capital city."

Mardee and Lola walked around after they had their lunch. They sat on the steps of the capitol and marveled at the impressive beauty of this building that housed our government. "It makes you feel so proud to be an American," Mardee said emotionally.

They visited the Lincoln Memorial and stood in awe in the shadow of the great man who sat there with a troubled and thoughtful expression on his marble face. They read his Gettysburg Address carved into the wall behind him. They stood in respectful silence. They realized the moment was too big for mere words.

The line was long, and they decided not to go up in the Washington Monument. "Maybe tomorrow," they promised themselves. They found a small shop and bought a dish of ice cream for their supper. They were too excited to be hungry.

They decided it was time to go back to the hotel and rest a while and then get ready to go out for the show. They put on their evening gowns and paraded back and forth for each other's approval.

"You look more elegant than the queen of England," Lola remarked as Mardee walked back and forth in her soft gray dress with her green hat and shoes. "And that's just the right dress for this hotel. Maybe they'll pay you to sit in the lobby and attract customers."

"If I run out of money, I may have to do that," Mardee said with a flirtatious smile.

Lola assumed the look of the beautiful star when she put on her garnet red gown. It set off to perfection her dark hair which cascaded down her back and accented her luminous dark eyes. Her full lips were painted deep red, and her olive cheeks were touched up with a soft glow of subtle rouge

"I should have left you at home," Mardee howled. "You are going to put me in the shade wherever we go."

"No one has ever outshone you, Mardee," Lola said in a definite tone of voice. "I will make you only more gorgeous. I'm just happy to walk in your shadow."

Mardee put her arms impulsively around her friend. "I love you, Lola," she said, "and I'm so glad you are with me. Look out, our nation's capital; here come the girls from the Manzanos."

22

Mardee opened her eyes the next morning and gazed at the delicate pattern on the ceiling of her room. There's a garden up there, she thought, with flowers, fountains, and birds. She snuggled down into the soft covers of the bed and smiled as she thought of what the day would bring. "I'm going to see Carter today," she said softly. "Today is the day." She kept her voice down because Lola still lay in deep sleep beside her.

But first, we must address Congress, she reminded herself. I must speak in my most eloquent tones today as I stand up for the right of American women to vote. That won't be hard to do, because I really believe what I'll be saying.

Mardee stretched her body languidly between the sheets. How nice to be lazy and not have a demanding time schedule calling the steps constantly. I don't remember when I could just lie in bed and do nothing. She knew this was a true statement. Ever since her grandmother had died when she was twelve years old, she had been getting up early every morning to face her chores of the day.

She closed her eyes and thought back to their first evening in the big city. They had dressed in their evening clothes and waited in the lobby for Rupert to pick them up at six o'clock. He had been right on the minute, and took them to the car parked in front. "I'm taking you to Ford's Theater," he informed them, "where you will join Miss Reynolds."

"Ford's Theater," Mardee had said in a low voice to Lola. "That's where President Lincoln was assassinated." Lola had looked back at her with large anxious eyes.

It took only a few minutes before the vehicle slowed down and parked in front of a big impressive building. As the two young women followed Rupert up the stairs to the interior, Mardee remembered whispering to Lola, "Don't forget: head up, shoulders back, and smile."

Rupert had led Mardee and Lola past the first floor and up more steps to the private boxes. He then pushed back maroon curtains and told them to enter. Mardee stepped hesitantly through the entrance, and as her eyes adjusted to the light, she saw a lone woman standing in the box with the stage and rows of seats in the background. Jeanette Reynolds stepped forward and extended her hand in greeting. "Welcome to Washington, DC and Ford's Theater," she had said pleasantly. "It's so good to see you in these surroundings."

"Saying we are thrilled to be here is an understatement," Mardee had exclaimed. For once, words escaped her, and she was thankful for the easy conversation Miss Reynolds initiated and kept going.

Miss Reynolds had pointed to a box near theirs which was draped in gold curtains. "That is the presidential box where Mr. Lincoln was shot," she said in a low intense voice. "He lived until the next morning."

Miss Reynolds alleviated the seriousness of the conversation by pointing out other boxes and current celebrities. "There is President and Mrs. Wilson," she said, and Mardee and Lola gazed in awe at the profile of the president.

"He looks older than I imagined," Mardee said.

"This war has taken its toll on him," Miss Reynolds remarked. "It is rumored that his health is not good."

Mardee remembered the excitement she felt in her chest when the heavy curtains started to open, and the lights dimmed. Soon she was lost in the action on the stage. The plot of the play was similar to most of the stage performances she had seen. The beautiful daughter of a wealthy man was being pursued by a charming villain. Just when it appeared that he would have the girl and all her father's money, the unassuming hero foiled his plot and won the girl's heart.

"All's well that ends well," Miss Reynolds said as she rose to lead them out of their box. "I was hoping tonight's story would be a little more thought provoking."

"It was wonderful," Lola said as the theater lights shone flatteringly upon her animated face.

"You could do that," Mardee said to Lola. "You could do an even more striking performance."

"She's certainly beautiful enough to be a star," Miss Reynolds commented.

"Someday she'll be on Broadway," Mardee prophesied.

"I think you are right," Miss Reynolds said sagely. Lola's cheeks were bright red with excitement at the compliments.

What a wonderful time our first evening in the capital city was, Mardee said to herself as she curled her body into the softness of her bed. Of course, when Miss Reynolds told me she had made arrangements for me to visit with Carter the next afternoon, I was too happy to even thank her. I must do that today.

The thought of the coming events caused Mardee to jump out of bed and get her speech out of her briefcase. She walked up and down the plush carpet in front of the full length mirror as she practiced the speech. She had it almost memorized and only glanced at her paper occasionally. As she watched her smiling face in the mirror, she realized her delivery was impressive. She closed her speech with just the right amount of confidence, tempered with humility. "And so, I implore you, Honorable Congress men and women of the United States, to vote with your hearts and your intelligence and give the women of this great country the right to vote in the next election in 1920."

Mardee turned around to see Lola sitting up in bed, watching and listening to her with a smile on her face. "You think you are going to charm all the old men into voting for this bill," she said with a giggle.

"If I don't get the job done, you will," Mardee said confidently. "Now you had better practice."

Lola jumped out of bed. "I'm going to concentrate more on how I look than on what I say," she said pertly. "There's more than one way to skin a cow, as my old daddy used to say."

The young women, dressed impressively in their new outfits, climbed back into Rupert's limousine to be taken to the congressional chambers. Although they carried themselves with poise as they entered this powerful room, their eyes were shifting nervously from the rows of pompous elected officials to the intimidating man who stood in the front of the chanber at a high impressive desk where he wielded a gavel with impassioned strength. They were led to seats near the front to await their turn at the lectern.

A portly gentleman was speaking in a monotonous voice, and Mardee looked around at the congressmen. Some were interested in what the speaker was saying, and some were openly paying no attention. Some were whispering among themselves, some were gazing off into space, and one man was reading a newspaper. Mardee felt the urge to giggle at the different attitudes of these important lawmakers, but she stifled her impulse. She knew she must do nothing to antagonize these people if she were going to win them over to her views. As she analyzed the situation and formulated her plans, she found herself becoming very calm in her determination to effectively state her cause.

Jeanette Reynolds had risen and walked briskly to the podium. She faced the legislative room and after a brief pause started her introduction of Mardee. "We have a guest speaker today who hails from the great state of New Mexico," she began. "I had the good fortune to meet her when I traveled in the southwest a few months ago. I was very impressed with this young woman.

"Mardee Spencer McMahan was born in New Mexico when it was still a territory. Her father migrated west from Illinois and stopped for a while to hunt buffalo in Kansas. He left Dodge City to go on to Oklahoma when he joined the land rush in that state. Then he moved on farther west to settle land and build a thriving lumber business in the mountains of New Mexico. His wife became the postmistress in Eastview, New Mexico, and she also taught the mountain school for the area children, as well as took care of her own family. Mardee helped her mother with all these chores.

"Sarah Spencer, Mardee's mother, never voted in an election in spite of the facts that she established a post office and ran it and taught many years in a one room school. Does it make sense that a woman of this caliber was not allowed to vote?

"Sarah Spencer's daughter is here today to talk to you about a woman's right to vote. She has worked long and hard in northern New Mexico to educate people on this issue and has brought thousands of signatures for our consideration when this issue comes up for a vote. She is going to talk to us now and describe how the women of New Mexico feel about being given the right to vote. Gentlemen, I have the distinct honor of introducing our speaker of the hour, Mardee Spencer McMahan. Please give Mardee a big welcome."

Mardee walked to the front of the room, and she felt as if she were in a dream. This can't be real, she was thinking. I must be dreaming. But when she stopped at the podium and faced the big room of many congressmen and one lone congresswoman, she knew this was, indeed, absolutely real. They were all looking at her very intently, and she paused for a long minute returning the look. In her mind she was willing their interest. You will listen to me, and you will pay attention, she silently promised. And if you, sir, pick up that paper again, I will walk back there and tear it out of your hands.

Mardee broke the stillness of the room and said, "I thank you, Miss Reynolds, for that introduction and the tribute you paid to my father and my mother. Both of them were intrepid pioneers, and I am proud to follow in their footsteps. They, and the people like them, are the ones who pushed back the western frontier for us. They were people who never stopped working for progress, and we must model ourselves after their philosophy very seriously. But they didn't win all the battles for us. Now it's time for us to take up our armor and continue the good fight of our ancestors.

"I went to work for the first governor of the state of New Mexico, the Honorable William McDonald, when I was barely eighteen years of age. I did general office chores and served as his official interpreter. I also went to school part time and worked for my room and board and taught some Spanish children to read at the same time I was working for the governor. Honorable Congressmen and Honorable Congresswoman Reynolds, I could work for the governor, but I couldn't vote for him. Does that make any sense? As my father would say, 'There's something wrong with this picture.'"

Mardee paused and smiled charismatically in the direction of her audience. She was willing them to give her a hand, and sure enough, the clapping started.

"Thank you so much," Mardee continued after the applause subsided. Then she continued, "I have been working for two years on the Woman's Suffrage Movement. I have enjoyed taking the message of freedom and equality to my sisters in New Mexico, and this message has been well received.

"I could tell you of the many experiences I have had as I have worked for this movement. I'm sure you will be interested to know how strongly the women of New Mexico feel about this constitutionally implied right. I could tell you all about how they feel on this subject, but I think I've thought of a better way to share it with you. I have brought from New Mexico a woman who has worked with me in this crusade. She has helped me with the petitions, and she has interpreted for me. She is half Mexican, and she has been a great help in teaching her people the importance of this right. So, Lola Tompkins has traveled here to Washington, DC with me to add her voice to this call for your consideration of women's rights. Lola is an outstanding woman who comes from the mountains of New Mexico originally, but she now lives in Santa Fe where she acts and sings for the Santa Fe Drama Company. She is the toast of Santa Fe, and it is my pleasure to give you the beautiful and talented Lola Tompkins who will talk to you for a few minutes."

As Lola rose to walk to the front of the crowd, which was no longer lethargic and uninterested, she received an enthusiastic welcome. All eyes were on the graceful girl as she took her place behind the podium. Mardee knew she was responding to them just as she would to an adoring audience at one of her plays. She lowered her head in an imperceptible bow and then raised it, revealing an irresistible smile radiating over everyone.

"My dear friends," Lola spoke in clear tones, "I thank you so much for this honor. To stand here before you in this fabulous center of our government is more than a poor mountain girl could ever think would happen to her in her wildest dreams.

"I thank you for this opportunity, and I beg you earnestly to vote for the bill that will give us women in New Mexico and all over the United States our right to vote.

"And, I invite you to Santa Fe to enjoy our fair city and to come to see our creative efforts at the New Mexico Drama Company. I will personally give you a tour of our capital and arrange passes for you to see our play production."

Lola smiled prettily and walked down from the podium to thunderous applause. She waved a dainty hand, first to one side of the room, and then to the other, and her smile seemed to be meant personally for each person in the room.

Mardee, who had stepped back behind Lola while she spoke, again faced the crowd from the podium and said, when it was finally quiet enough to speak, "So, in conclusion, I would like to thank Miss Jeanette Reynolds so much for inviting us to come to speak to you. Miss Reynolds, you know you are our hero. And, everyone is invited to come to see us in the Land of Enchantment. New Mexico will seduce you with its unique beauty, and its people will win your hearts and souls forever. Hasta Luego, mis amigos. Until we meet again."

Mardee started back to her seat, and the audience rose as one in a standing ovation. Mardee took Lola's hand and whispered, "We did it, Lola. We got their votes." Lola only smiled innocently and turned to clap her hands as if in applause for the congressional group. She waved to the crowd in the balcony and threw kisses to them.

Ever the actress, Mardee thought. Ever the actress, condescending to recognize her admirers.

Jeanette Reynolds rose from her place and came to stand by Mardee and Lola. "Wonderful speeches, ladies," she said in a soft voice. "I think that vote is assured now."

Mardee, Lola, and Jeanette Reynolds faced the crowd with magnanimous smiles of appreciation. They knew they had won for their cause.

Miss Reynolds put her arm around Mardee and whispered into her ear, "Rupert will take you to the Walter Reed Hospital to see your husband now. Good luck, my dear."

23

Rupert stopped the limousine in front of the Shamrock Hotel, and Lola pressed Mardee's hand tightly until the door was opened for her to get out. "Good luck," she mouthed, and blew a kiss at the departing vehicle.

"How far is the hospital?" Mardee asked when Rupert got back in the car.

"Not far," he said crisply. "We will be there shortly."

Mardee sat back and breathed deeply to settle her fluttering heart. Palpitations? she wondered. Mother Spencer often had complained of "palpitations of the heart" when she became nervous or upset. But her thoughts turned quickly to Carter.

"God, please let his condition be improved," she prayed softly. "Please let there be hope that he can recover completely."

Raising her voice, she said, "Please tell me about the hospital, Rupert. I don't know anything about it."

Rupert cleared his throat and said as he turned the car north on Seventh Avenue, "This hospital started operations in 1909. It was called Walter Reed General Hospital in honor of Major Walter Reed, an Army physician who discovered that mosquitoes transmit yellow fever. It started out as an eighty bed facility, but they expanded it during the war to take care of the casualties coming back here. It cares for many service men, as well as members of congress and the president and vice president. Medical research is also done here."

Mardee opened her eyes wide in awe and said, "It sounds as if they should be able to help my husband."

Rupert turned left off the street and started up a wide driveway. An imposing three story building stood in the near distance. The limousine circled around a lovely fountain and up to the front of the columned entrance.

"Here you are, Mrs. McMahan," Rupert announced. "You will be allowed to stay for one hour. I will return and pick you up here at noon."

Only an hour? Mardee questioned as she walked up the immaculate stone steps and pulled the huge glass door open. I'll see about that. She walked to the reception desk and said in a halting voice that she would like to see Lieutenant McMahan.

The receptionist looked up at Mardee with impersonal eyes and asked, "What is your name?"

"I am Mardee McMahan. I am his wife."

"Oh," the girl said with more interest. "Let me check with the nurse on his floor."

As the girl rang up the nurse, Mardee looked around at the huge waiting room filled with chairs and benches. Several people sat there quietly with serious expressions of their faces. She vaguely wondered if they were waiting to get in the hospital or were waiting to visit someone who was a patient.

The receptionist put the phone down and said, "You may take the elevator up to the third floor. Mr. McMahan's room is number 304. Have a good visit with your husband." The girl smiled and pointed to the elevator.

Mardee took a deep breath and got on the elevator to take her ride to see her husband. Her legs felt wooden, and her finger felt lifeless as she pressed the number three. Am I really here, or am I dreaming? she asked herself.

Room 304 was close to the elevator exit. The door was cracked open, and she paused and knocked gently. She heard a well-remembered voice say, "Come on in."

Mardee pushed the door open slowly and looked toward the tall bed in the corner. A man sat propped up on two pillows, and in spite of his long hair and black beard, she knew she was face to face with Carter. His arms were extended, and a big smile cut through the whiskers. "Mardee, darlin'" were the words she heard.

All hesitation vanished, and she ran quickly to the bed and felt herself enveloped in the embrace she loved so well. The months of anxiety and uncertainty were wiped away in the long passionate kiss which followed. But, in spite of her jubilation of being held in Carter's arms again, she was painfully aware of the thinness of his body as he pressed her close to his heart.

Then the tears came. Sobs from the depths of her being established the reality of this event. "I wasn't dreaming," she gulped between the tears. "You are here, and I'm here with you."

Carter patted her back and said in a calm voice, "Of course you're here, my precious. I've prayed for this moment so long." He lifted her head and said, "Let me look at you."

"I look terrible," Mardee sobbed. She pushed hopelessly at her hair and her tears.

"The most beautiful girl in the world," he said softly, "and you're all mine."

Mardee laid her head back on Carter's chest, and as he held her, the tears started abating. She lay there quietly a few minutes, and then she raised her head and said with a touch of her old feistiness, "After getting through the war, I'm trying to drown you in my tears." She stood up and added, "Besides, I'm ruining my new suit."

"Get a chair and pull it up as close as you can," Carter directed. "We've got lots to talk about."

Mardee came directly to the point after she seated herself and took Carter's hand. "Tell me about your injuries." She looked straight into his dark eyes and asked, "Is there damage to your eyes?"

"There is some damage," Carter said. "But the specialists here are hoping to keep it contained to a minimum."

"Can you see me?" Mardee asked anxiously.

"Oh yes," Carter replied with a teasing smile. "Who could miss that green hat?"

"You don't like my hat," Mardee said in a disappointed voice

"I love your green hat," Carter reassured her. "But my vision is somewhat blurred, and I don't see well in the distance at all. My doctor says that strong glasses will correct most of my problems."

"That's wonderful," Mardee said with relief. She had worried the most about Carter's eyesight.

"My body received minimal burning," Carter continued. "My helmet and beard protected my head and face. My uniform protected the rest of my body." Carter paused momentarily and then added, "But there is some damage to my lungs."

"Is it serious damage?" Mardee asked with dread in her voice. "It must be, or you wouldn't be here."

"Yes, it is not good," Carter said. Then he added quickly, "But I'm better since I've been here. They are trying some new medicine on me that seems to be helping."

Mardee pushed the thought of damaged lungs aside. Unconsciously she knew she didn't want to pursue this subject, and she said with a lilt in her voice, "Now I must tell you about everything that has happened since you've been gone."

Carter sighed and leaned back on his pillows. "Tell me everything, darlin'. Don't quit talking. I love to hear your voice." He closed his eyes in perfect contentment.

Mardee knew she had written everything that had happened in detail, but she didn't know if all her letters had gotten to him. So, she started with the arrival of a pregnant Lola and told her story, from the delivery of the baby boy to her successful theater career. "I can't wait for you to see Robbie Blue," she said. "You will love him."

"As you obviously do," Carter said. He opened his eyes and stole a quick look at Mardee.

Then Mardee brought Carter up to date on the law office. She concluded by saying, "The law firm is doing well. Will spends many extra hours there to assure the success of the firm. I have spent all the time I can there, also, and we hired Raquel Riley to be there when I was in school. Recently we hired Jeff Corbin to do some part time work. Will was just snowed under with all the cases. Jeff is an expert in Spanish Land Grant and Indian Reservation Law, and we needed his expertise in these areas. He has worked out well."

"Jeff Corbin?" Carter asked. "Have I heard you talk about him?"

"Probably," Mardee said quickly. "I've known him since I was a young girl. He is an old friend of Papa's. He helped me get my job with the governor."

"Oh yes," Carter said. He opened his eyes again and directed a searching glance at Mardee. "Now I remember."

"I hoped you would approve of our hiring him," Mardee said, speaking her words in a faster meter than usual.

"I'm sure you've done fine," Carter said with a sweep of his hand as if brushing away any doubts. "You have finished your law courses by now?" he asked.

"I'm all done," Mardee said proudly "I'll take my test in the spring."

"I knew you would do it," Carter said quietly. "The first female law graduate in the state. I'm married to a celebrity."

"If I'm a celebrity, it's because I'm married to Lieutenant Carter McMahan, war hero," Mardee corrected him.

The nurse came in at this moment in her starched white uniform, sporting her practiced smile. "Visiting hours are over, Mrs. McMahon," she said.

Mardee looked helplessly at Carter, and he said, "You can come back at seven o'clock tonight for another visit. I'll get some rest now, and I'll see you later."

Mardee reluctantly kissed Carter's lips and turned to go. She glanced back as she went out the door, and caught her breath for a moment as she noticed the pained expression on his face. He's hurting more than he is telling me, she thought. And when he held me, his body felt so thin. But she shook her anxieties aside and went down the hall more confidently than when she had entered the hospital. "He's alive, and it's so good to see him," she whispered reassuringly to herself.

24

Mardee had been in the hospital room only a few minutes in the evening when Carter's doctor stepped in to visit with them. He introduced himself and looked Mardee over with honest curiosity and admiration. "Lieutenant McMahan has talked about his beautiful wife, and I'll have to admit he is not exaggerating," he said in a deep voice. He took her extended hand and squeezed it earnestly. "I'm so glad you could come to see our patient. That should help him to recover faster. I am Doctor Wintergreen."

Mardee's spirits were lifted as she watched the doctor examine her husband. He seemed so knowledgeable and sure of his movements as he listened to his breathing and his heartbeat and took his blood pressure. Finally, he said, "You're sounding better today. Your heartbeat is a little fast, but that is to be expected with your special visitor here." As the doctor walked out of the room, he said to Mardee, "Stop by my office on your way out. I would like to have a little chat with you."

This last visit with Carter was overshadowed with the thought that Mardee would be leaving tomorrow to head back west, but the reunited husband and wife made good use of their limited time. Carter stroked the red-gold hair he loved so well and said, "When I get home, we'll both be working together in the law firm. We'll be together all the time, day and night."

"Nothing will ever make up for your being gone this last year," Mardee whispered.

"We'll find ways to make up for that lost time," Carter said with a smile. "I promise you, my pretty."

"Remember that sign you have to make," Mardee reminded him. "McMahan, Cabot, and Spencer."

"I'll get right to work on it," Carter assured her.

Carter asked about Mardee's parents, and she told him of her concerns for her father. "He's not that old," Carter reassured her. "That old mountain man will live forever."

Mardee nestled in Carter's arms, and they were both quiet as they drew into their own thoughts. She felt so safe as she nestled in his protecting embrace. "I can't leave you," Mardee finally whispered.

"We do what we have to do in this world," Carter said consolingly. "We climb one mountain and then get ready for the next one. I think we have all the high ones climbed, though, and we can get across the next one easily."

"I know," she said, and then with a toss of her head she added, "We'll climb that next mountain, you bet. We'll climb it together, and we'll never be alone again."

"That's my girl," Carter said as he drew her in his arms for a last kiss. But Mardee felt his strong arms starting to falter. She knew he was tired.

"I'm going, darling," she said swiftly, while she still had control of her emotions. "I'm going to talk to the doctor. Then I'll go to the hotel to pack and get ready to leave. We catch the nine o'clock train this evening for New York City."

Carter said nothing, but he looked longingly into her eyes. "I'll be with you soon, I hope."

Mardee noticed that his eyes were beginning to droop. She knew he would soon go to sleep. She bent over and gave him one more passionate kiss and turned and walked quickly out of the room and down the hall. As she passed the nurse's station, she asked for directions to the doctor's office.

Dr. Wintergreen helped Mardee to a chair and faced her across his desk. "I thought I should be very frank with you concerning your husband's condition," he said by way of starting their conversation. "I planned to write you, but since you are here, it will be better to talk with you in person. And, I don't have time to write a letter, anyway."

"Yes, I'm sure you're very busy," Mardee said quietly. "I suppose there are many other soldiers here with problems besides Carter."

"Yes, too many," Dr. Wintergreen agreed. "But, as far as Lieutenant McMahan is concerned, his condition is a little more difficult to cope with than some. He actually survived the gas attack better than most do. At least, the eye damage is minimal, and there was no serious burning. However, there is some lung damage, and it is difficult to determine just how much. The x-rays don't show us serious damage, but his overall condition seems to be pretty weak. We wonder if there is something wrong we are not picking up. We plan on running more tests."

Mardee looked at the doctor and felt completely speechless. She just didn't know what to say, since she was so unfamiliar with medical problems. She noticed the doctor's eyes had dark circles under them, and there were lines of weariness in his face. Working with ill people all the time must be difficult, she thought. I don't think I could do it.

"Anyway," Dr. Wintergreen continued with a tinge of hope in his voice, "we are trying some new medicine with him, and he seems to be responding. If his improvement continues, we can send him home within the month, I think."

In spite of her inactive brain, Mardee understood those words. "That's wonderful," she said ecstatically. "Oh, thank you, doctor. Thank you for everything."

Dr. Wintergreen rose and came around his desk and took both her hands in his. "I sincerely hope he comes along well. We'll do all we can for him, and then we'll send him home to you, and to God." He looked deep into her trusting blue-green eyes and added, "Good luck, my dear."

Mardee walked toward the door of the hospital and suddenly felt an overwhelming impulse to run back to see Carter one more time. She stopped in her tracks, but then forced her body to go blindly through the hospital door and hastily get into the limousine waiting for her. She felt as if she were in a strange trancelike condition. She experienced no emotions nor pain. She just felt removed from her situation. I'm here in body but not in spirit, she thought. I wonder when I'll come back to earth.

Rupert dropped Mardee at her hotel door and told her he would be back a little after eight o'clock to take her to the train. Mardee mumbled her thanks and added; "Now I've got to climb that next mountain." Rupert nodded his head politely and turned back to his car. He hadn't understood what she had said, but he wasn't paid to understand people.

"I'll grab a bite and then take the two women to the train." He spoke aloud as he turned the car away from the hotel. His day's work was thankfully nearly done.

"I have you all packed," Lola said brightly as Mardee entered the hotel room. "Let's go down to the restaurant and have one last Irish supper. I'm going to miss this place."

"All right," Mardee said tonelessly. "That's fine with me."

Lola chattered to the waitress and the other customers sitting close to their table. She told them she loved being in the east and hoped to come back and stay longer in New York City some day. Mardee ignored her talk and concentrated on her conversation with Dr. Wintergreen. Did he give me hope or not? she wondered. I don't really know, she concluded. But one thing she did know for sure was that she was happy to be going back home. Lola could talk positively about the east all she wanted. Mardee knew she was very happy to be going home to the west.

The two young women boarded their train and waved goodbye to Jeanette Reynolds who had come with Rupert this time to see them off. She thanked them effusively for their help in getting the women's rights bill passed. As Mardee smiled and expressed her appreciation to Miss Reynolds for all her help and hospitality, she was aware of her sudden realization that she had no interest in this bill at the moment, and didn't care if she ever got to vote. She had more important matters on her mind.

Then their porter came and took them directly to the Pullman car where their berths were located. They would rest there until they changed trains in New York City in the middle of the night. Mardee pulled her blanket over her head and prayed the movement of the train would soon lull her into a thankful sleep. She knew that seeing Carter had been a wonderful thing for both of them, but she also realized that seeing him in this emaciated condition only multiplied her concerns. The more she thought about the doctor's words, the more she detected warnings in them. I think he was trying to prepare me for the worst, she worried. Still, she reminded herself, he said he thought the medicine was helping him. She tossed and turned, and she knew she was developing a sick headache. She kept repeating to herself every word of her conversations with Carter and with the doctor. Trying to talk herself into drifting into sleep, she told the faint lights of the town in the distance, "By the time I get back to Santa Fe I'll be better able to figure out this dilemma, and maybe I can also figure out a way to cope with the future."

25

Mardee gazed toward the hills of Trinidad as their train swiftly left them behind. "We'll be in New Mexico soon," she told Lola. "We've got the Raton Pass left to climb over, and then we'll head for the Sangre de Cristos and old Santa Fe. It's going to be good to get home."

Lola said nothing for a few minutes as she watched the Colorado landscape disappear. Her expression was one of deep thought. Finally, she sat up erectly in her seat and cleared her throat before she said, "Mardee, we have to talk."

Mardee turned her eyes in the direction of her friend. She felt exhausted and didn't relish the prospect of doing much talking. Especially, she didn't want to talk seriously, and from the looks of Lola's demeanor, this was going to be a serious conversation.

"What is it, Lola?" she asked in a resigned voice.

"I need to tell you about a decision I have made," Lola said in a halting, but determined tone of voice. "I'm planning on leaving Santa Fe in the near future."

"Mardee straightened up in surprise. "Where are you going?" she asked. All Mardee's lethargy had suddenly vanished.

"I'm going east," Lola said in a firmer voice. "I want to try my luck on Broadway."

"You can't do that by yourself," Mardee protested. "New York City is huge. You would be totally lost there."

"I won't be by myself," Lola said. "Jetson Spangler will be with me."

"Oh," Mardee said in an incredulous voice. "Are you telling me that you are running off with Jet?"

"I'm not running off," Lola protested. "We'll finish our current production, and then we will both resign from the company and head east." She lifted her head and her small chin pointed out defensively.

"Jet has friends in New York City?" Mardee asked. "I remember him talking about some friends visiting him who were in the acting business."

"That's right," Lola said in a strained voice. "He feels he can get work quickly in the city, and he may be able to help me land something in the big-time."

This is what he is telling her, Mardee thought. But how much of all these plans will work out? Aloud, she said, "I just don't know about this, Lola. What if things don't go the way you hope?"

"I have faith in Jet, and I have faith in myself," Lola answered. "Jet knows show business, and I know I have talent."

"Of course you do," Mardee said as she impulsively grabbed Lola's hands and squeezed them. "You've got more singing and acting talent than anyone I've ever seen. And, certainly you are very beautiful." In her mind she knew those were probably the reasons Jet was taking her east. If he couldn't get work, he could manage her career.

Lola's pretty face crumpled, and she looked at Mardee with teary, appealing eyes. "I love him, Mardee, and I think he loves me. Together, I'm sure we can make it. And I want it so much, Mardee. I've got the feel of the stage in my heart, and I can't be without it."

Suddenly Mardee knew Lola would make it on the stage. Some unknown voice told her it would happen. She had everything she needed to make it happen. But she wasn't so sure about Jet's continued presence in the picture. She had always sensed something mysterious and a little deceitful about him.

"Are you going to marry Jet?" she asked.

"No," Lolo answered without hesitation.. "He's married to a woman who is ill and in a sanitarium back east. He says he won't divorce her because of her condition. But I don't care if I'm married to him or not. I love him, and I want to be with him."

So that was it, Mardee thought. He's married. I knew there was something about him that he wasn't revealing. Then a pang shot through her heart as she thought of the baby. "What about Robbie Blue?" she asked in a panicky voice. "What are your plans for him?"

Lola swallowed hard in an obvious effort to answer Mardee's question. "That's the other thing I need to talk to you about." She gulped and said the words very fast, . "I would like for you to take care of him."

"You would leave him with me?" Mardee asked in a doubtful voice.

"Yes," Lola said quietly.

"Well," Mardee said slowly, "of course I will take care of him. I love him very much, you know."

"Yes, I know," Lola said almost sadly, "and he loves you, too. You are the one he looks to when he has a problem. You sense his needs and take care of them much better than I."

"That isn't true," Mardee protested. "He will miss his mother very much."

"But, he's young," Lola continued in the same sad voice. "He will forget me."

"You'll be coming back to see him often, won't you?" Mardee asked. This conversation was becoming almost unreal to her. She couldn't believe what she was hearing.

"I hope I can come back to see him," Lola said. "But I really don't know what is going to happen regarding my career. So I can't truthfully say how often I'll be able to see him."

Lola's eyes filled with tears, and she dug in her purse for a hankie. She wiped her cheeks and blew her nose and then turned resolutely to Mardee again. "I want you to take him permanently, Mardee. I can't take care of him and have a career, too. He'll be better off with you in Santa Fe where he is with people who love him. I couldn't bear to leave him with strangers in a big city."

"Of course I'll take care of him," Mardee repeated again. "I'm sure Addie will continue to help me with him. But I don't want you to lose your son permanently."

"I won't lose him if you have him, Mardee. I know you would always share him with me."

"Of course," Mardee said brokenly. "He'll always be your son."

"You and I will know that," Lola said, "but what I really want you to do is to adopt him and raise him as your own son. I want him to have the Spencer family behind him, and I want him to have all the advantages you and your family can give him."

"My father loves him already," Mardee said with a smile. Her eyes were luminous, and she felt the depression that had engulfed her since leaving Washington, D.C growing lighter. Deep down, she was pleased with this development. She instinctively knew she would have a very difficult time if Lola took the baby away from her.

"I'll make one stipulation," Lola said, "before I will sign adoption papers. He will go by the name of Robert Benjamin Spencer." Lola emphasized the last name and looked Mardee resolutely in the eyes, and there was no doubt she was serious about this request.

"I probably would want him to have my married name," Mardee said slowly.

"No," Lola said firmly. "I want him to be raised as a Spencer. And, after all, you are still a Spencer, even though you are married."

"That's true," Mardee said thoughtfully. "We'll think about this, Lola. If you still feel the same way when you get ready to leave, we'll legalize the adoption the way you want it."

"Thanks," Lola said as she heaved a big sigh and lay back in her seat. She closed her eyes to wrestle with her own thoughts, and Mardee knew she didn't want to talk any more at this time.

Mardee closed her own eyes, and the cherubic picture of Robbie Blue Eyes danced in front of her. His chubby fists reached out toward her, and his blue eyes twinkled while he blew bubbles and smiled until his dimples peeked through. My son, she thought hesitantly and then jubilantly. My own son! She wanted to shout this news to the world!

Jeff met the weary travelers when they got off the train in Lamy. When Mardee stepped onto New Mexico soil again, a great sense of relief surged through her. Although she felt unsure of her steps because, even though the train had stopped, she still seemed to be swaying over the country on the endless ride. But she suddenly felt safe and grounded again as she carefully descended the short steel stairs. She had seen Jeff's smiling face from the train window, and knowing he was there to take them home added to her feeling of security. He greeted both women and took their suitcases.

"Welcome home, ladies," he said. The delighted note in his voice added to their feelings of a happy homecoming.

A small bundle of energy attached itself to Mardee's legs. "Hello, ladies," a musical voice trilled. Mardee looked down into the smiling face of Beth.

"How nice that you came to meet us," Mardee said in pleased surprise. She gave the little girl a big hug.

After a moment, Beth protested sweetly, "Don't hug too tight, Mrs. McMahan."

"I'm sorry darling," Mardee said. "I'll turn you over to Lola. Maybe she won't hug so hard."

"I would have brought Robbie Blue," Jeff said apologetically to Lola, "but he was in the middle of his nap."

"That's all right," Lola said with a catch in her voice.

Mardee noted the look of pain that swiftly crossed Lola's face. She knew the joyful homecoming was shadowed by momentous changes that were soon to come.

26

The days after coming home from the Washington, DC trip were busy. Mardee had to catch up on a backlog of work at the office, and Lola was preparing to leave. She insisted that adoption papers be drawn up immediately, so Mardee had instructed Will to do that transaction according to her wishes. The papers had been signed and filed in the court house. Also, the Christmas holidays were near, and decorating and present-buying were necessary chores.

Mardee walked up to her front door at the end of the day with arms loaded with Christmas presents and struggled with the lock. "Drat!" she said as she dropped the key and had to set down the packages in order to retrieve it. She opened the door and walked into the house with a scowl on her face. As she set the parcels down, she noticed a note on the table. It was brief, and her eyes scanned it swiftly.

"Mardee dear," she read, "We are leaving today. Thanks for everything. I'll write you soon and let you know how things are going for Jet and me. I love you, Lola. P.S. You'll have to pick up Robbie Blue after work. Give him big kisses for me Please tell George goodbye for me."

Mardee sat down heavily on a kitchen chair. "She's gone already. She's really gone," she said sadly. "That's why she was in such a hurry to get those papers finalized." She sat for only a moment and then hastily put her groceries away. Then she got back in the car and drove to Addie's house to get Robbie.

Addie opened the door to Mardee, holding the baby in her arms. Mardee's face told her something was wrong. "What is it, dear?" she asked with concern in her voice.

"Lola's gone," Mardee said quietly. "She's gone with Jetson Spangler. They are going to try their fortune in New York City."

"And you get to keep the baby for her?" Addie asked, her eyes round with disbelief.

"The baby is mine," Mardee said flatly. "She wanted me to have him."

Addie was silent as she looked away thoughtfully. "Well," she finally said. "that may be for the best—for all of you."

"It's certainly the best for me," Mardee said as she reached for Robbie and planted a kiss on his cherubic cheek. As she reached for the bag that held his diapers and bottles, she added, "I'm taking some time off for Christmas. I may go home to the ranch for the holidays, so I won't be bringing the baby tomorrow. I'll talk to you later about my definite plans."

Mardee headed out the door which Addie held open for her. Then as Addie walked to the gate with her, Mardee asked, "Do you really think it's all right for me to have Robbie Blue?"

"You'll do a wonderful job with him," Addie said emphatically.

"I'll let Lola see him whenever she wants to," Mardee said, as if trying to further convince Addie that it was right for her to have the baby.

"I'm sure you will," Addie said, and then changed the subject, "Have you heard from Carter lately?"

"Just one letter," Mardee said. "He said he wasn't feeling too well. He thought he was getting a cold. I hope he doesn't get this horrible flu that is going around."

Addie opened the gate and then held the car door for Mardee. As Mardee drove off, she noticed the serious expression on Addie's face. She worries too much, she thought.

The house seemed very quiet that evening after Mardee put Robbie to bed. She felt at loose ends and sat down to write Carter a letter. She ended up writing several pages. "I need to talk to someone tonight," she wrote, "and you are the chosen one." She told him of Lola's leaving and consequently, her first evening alone with Robbie Blue. "He's so cuddly and bright and happy," she wrote. "I can't wait until you're home to enjoy him. He'll be good medicine for you."

Mardee ended her letter by confirming her love for her husband and thanking him for all the joy he had brought her. "I'm the luckiest woman in the world to have you," she wrote. "I can climb any mountain with you by my side."

Mardee felt better after her letter visit with Carter, and she went to bed after checking Robbie. "I don't have to work tomorrow," she told herself aloud. "I will sleep and rest all day." A small voice argued that would not be the case with the baby there, but she pushed every thought aside and needed sleep soon claimed her stressed and fatigued body.

The baby's fussing woke her up at the usual time the next morning. When she went to his crib, he looked up at her with a big smile and then continued sucking vigorously on his thumb. "Poor baby, you're hungry," she said. She picked him up to change him and carried him on one arm while she fixed a bottle with warm water from the reservoir on the end of the wood cook stove. As she sat in the rocking chair feeding him, she enjoyed every noisy drink of milk he rapidly sucked down his throat. "You're a piggly wiggly," she said lovingly. "You were a starved boy. Marmee should have been up feeding you sooner." She realized she had invented the name she would have the boy call her, "Marmee," she repeated. "That's a good name."

Robbie worked hard on finishing the contents of the bottle and looked up at Mardee with alert eyes. He waved his fists in the air and suddenly focused in on one of them. As he gazed admiringly at the hand, Mardee laughed with joyful abandon, "You're such a smart boy. You have found your own hand for the first time!"

The sound of a loud vehicle horn burst through Mardee's tender reflections of the baby. She set his emptied bottle down and rose to look out the door. Her father and his lumber truck had pulled up in front of her house. She opened the door and ran out to greet him

"Papa!" she yelled happily.

Ben Spencer waved back at his approaching daughter.

"I'm so glad you're here," she said as he opened his door to get out. "You're early, though. You must have left home about four o'clock."

"You're right," Ben said as he stretched his arms over his head. "It's been a long ride, but I wanted to get here early and unload and head back this afternoon. Have you got some breakfast for a hungry traveler?"

"I can make some," Mardee said in a pleased tone of voice. "Take your grandson, Papa Ben, and I'll cook some food."

Ben took the baby and looked fondly into his face. "Did I hear you say something about my grandson?" he asked tentatively.

"Yes, you did," Mardee said merrily. "Lola has gone back east with her director. They are going to try to get work there, and she left the baby with me. He's mine, Papa."

"You mean he's yours while she's gone," Ben corrected his daughter.

"No Papa," Mardee said firmly. "He's mine for all the time. I have adopted him legally."

Ben looked straight at his daughter, and detecting no deviation in her expression from her stated words, he said slowly, "In that case, I guess I am a grandfather." A big smile slowly spread over his face.

"Yes, you're Papa Ben," Mardee said happily.

The pungent smell of coffee soon permeated the house while Ben held the baby and entertained him. Mardee started frying bacon and eggs.

"How did you find Carter?" Ben called to Mardee in the kitchen.

"I guess he's making progress," Mardee called back. "His doctor told me they are using some new drugs on him they hope will help his lungs. I did hear from him this week, however, and he said he didn't feel that well. He was afraid he was getting a cold. Hopefully, it isn't the flue."

"That would be bad on his lungs," Ben agreed.

Ben and Mardee ate their breakfast, and Mardee put the baby down for his morning nap. Ben helped Mardee clear the table and told her he needed to take off to get his lumber unloaded.

"That's fine," Mardee said. "But stop by before you head back down the mountain. I'll have a lunch for you to eat on the way home."

Ben started out to his truck, and another vehicle drove up at that moment. The driver waved at Ben, and he shaded his eyes to see who got out of the car. It was Jeff, who walked briskly over to Ben and grabbed his hand in a hearty handshake. Mardee watched the men from her door and saw them stand in serious conversation for a few minutes.

"I wonder what they're talking about," she said aloud.

Just then the men turned and headed toward the house. There were apprehensive expressions on both their faces, and Mardee suddenly had a premonition of bad news. She opened the door and ran toward them. "What is it?" she asked anxiously. "What is wrong?"

Neither man answered, but Ben put his arm around her shoulders and looked deeply into her eyes. Jeff stood on the other side of her and grasped her arm firmly. "Tell me, Papa," Mardee demanded.

"It's about Carter," Ben said softly. "A telegram came to the law office this morning. Jeff took it for you and read it." Ben hesitated, and Mardee stamped her foot in frustration.

"Tell me," she repeated more loudly. Her eyes were agitated green diamonds as they took in Ben's anxious expression.

Jeff spoke at this moment. "The telegram was from Carter's doctor," he said.

"I know he hasn't been feeling very well," Mardee interrupted. "I got a letter from Carter yesterday."

Mardee's words hung in the air, and no one said anything for a moment. Finally, Ben continued his narration. "Carter unexpectedly died early this morning," Ben said in a low voice. "He developed pneumonia and went very fast. He couldn't fight this disease in his weakened condition."

Mardee stood as stiff as an inanimate object while her brain tried to decipher these words. She started to protest. "He can't," she whispered. Then her small body buckled, and she would have fallen to the ground had not the supporting arms caught her. Jeff picked her up and carried her into the house and laid her gently on the divan.

"She's fainted," Ben said. "I'll get a wet cloth to put on her forehead."

Jeff gently fanned the air around Mardee's inert body until Ben came back and wiped her face with a cool washcloth. "It's all right, Mardee girl," Ben kept saying. "Papa's here. I'll take care of you."

Mardee's eyes flickered open in a short time. She tried to sit up, but fell back weakly. "Lay still, Mardee," Jeff instructed her firmly. "You had a fainting spell, but you'll be all right. You must be very still for a while."

Mardee turned her head wearily to one side of her pillow and closed her eyes again. Slowly the tears started trickling down her pale cheeks. "Carter is gone?" she asked in a faint voice.

"Yes," Ben said. "I'm so sorry, Mardee."

Mardee lay very still while the slow tears rolled down her cheeks and Ben rinsed her face with the cool cloth. Jeff put his hand over her small hand and said tearfully, "I'm so sorry, Mardee. I would give anything if you didn't have to go through this. You've been so brave, Mardee. This should not happen to you."

"Life isn't always fair," Ben said sadly. Then with his usual talent for taking the lead in handling difficult situations, he said, "Let's get her to her bedroom, Jeff, so she can rest."

Jeff carried Mardee to her bed and laid her gently under the sheet and blanket Ben had turned back.

"I'll deliver my lumber and be back in a short while," Ben told Jeff. "Could you stay with her until I get back?"

"Of course," Jeff said. "I'll sit right here beside her."

"I hope the baby doesn't wake up," Ben said with an attempted smile. "I don't know if you know how to take care of babies."

"He knows," Mardee said suddenly, to the surprise of her father.

"Good," Ben said with relief. "I'll be back later, daughter." He patted her head and left.

Mardee knew her father was gone, and she knew Jeff was sitting beside her bed holding her hand. He seemed to realize she didn't want to talk. His only movement was to wipe her face with a soft handkerchief when the tears overflowed. Later she seemed to go into a drained sleep.

The baby started making purring noises from his crib two hours later, and Mardee stirred, also. "The baby needs fed," she said. "He needs a bottle."

"How do I make it?" Jeff asked.

"Get a clean bottle out of the cabinet," Mardee instructed. "Fill it half full of warm water from the reservoir and then pour in enough canned milk from the ice box to fill the bottle. You'll find clean nipples with the bottles."

Jeff went to the kitchen to fix the bottle for the baby. He followed Mardee's instructions and soon returned with a fresh bottle of milk. Mardee had removed the baby from his crib and sat in her bed holding him and talking to him. Jeff handed her the bottle, and the baby took it hungrily. Mardee's face and eyes looked red and swollen from her tears, but she seemed to be calm and in control of her emotions. She watched the baby eat and patted his little back while he concentrated on his food.

"He's such a good eater," she said in a proud voice. "and he never gets colic after he eats. He's such a good boy." She put him over her shoulder to persuade a burp out of his stomach before he continued with the rest of his food. "Burp for Marmee," she directed in a soft voice.

"That baby is the best thing in the world for you to have right now," Jeff said suddenly. "He'll keep your mind off your troubles while you take care of him."

"You're probably right," Mardee said in a sad voice. Then she lifted his tiny body up high and said, "This boy's smile would make anyone forget to cry. Right, Robbie Blue Eyes?"

Ben came in the door at that moment and looked relieved to see Mardee bouncing her baby boy up in the air and smiling at him. "I'll stay with her, Jeff," her father said. "Thanks for helping out."

"Glad I could do something," Jeff said. "But I really should go back to the office. Will Cabot will be out of his head holding things down by himself. Let me know if you need help with anything."

Ben walked with Jeff to the door. He shook hands with him and said, "They will probably be sending details to the office of when the body will be here. Let me know, and we will make the arrangements. I imagine the place for burial would be the Veteran's Cemetery here."

As Jeff started to walk off, Ben called, "Send a telegram to Sadie and tell her the sad news. Tell her to let the boys know. She can also let Floyd know if she has his address. He was fighting in Denver the last we heard from him. He might like to come down for the funeral. Tell her I'll let her know when the funeral is. I doubt she can come; she's too busy. But if you take care of that matter for me, it will help."

"Sure thing," Jeff called back. "I'll get right on it."

Ben turned back to the bedroom and reached out his hands for the baby. Mardee shook her head. "You don't want him, Papa. He needs a change in the worst way. I'll take care of that project, and you can have him when I get him cleaned up. Then he's yours for the rest of the afternoon while I rest and try to figure out what I'm going to do."

Ben looked sadly at his daughter's drawn face. It didn't seem very long ago that he and Sadie had comforted her after Frankie's death. As if reading his mind, Mardee asked, "Why does everyone I love leave me, Papa? You know this has happened before."

"Yes, and I don't know the answer any better now than I did before," Ben said quietly. "It doesn't seem fair. Carter was such an outstanding young man, and you never really had much time together. But the time you did have was quality time. You'll always have those happy memories."

Mardee shook her head hopelessly and sat up on the side of her bed holding the baby. "You'd better go in the other room, Papa." She saw his concerned look and said quickly, "I'll be fine. If I shed any tears they will be over this chore I have to do." She smiled faintly and reached for a clean diaper.

27

The funeral was over. Carter would sleep peacefully on a beautiful grassy knoll in the Veteran's Cemetery just outside Santa Fe. Mardee purposely arranged a short ceremony. The December wind was cold and cut through her clothes as she stood shivering while the Army Chaplain conducted the brief ceremony and the honorary gun salute cut sharply through the frosty air.

"A fitting place for him to rest," Mardee said to her father after the last prayer was spoken, and the small crowd turned to leave the cemetery. She firmly grasped her father's arm and walked with him toward her car. Her brother, Floyd, caught up with them and took Mardee's other arm.

Floyd opened the door for Mardee while Ben walked around the car to the driver's seat. Mardee turned her somber eyes up to Floyd. "Thanks for coming," she said. "I wish you could have known him. You would have liked him."

"I'm sure I would have," Floyd responded.

"Do you have to leave immediately?" Mardee asked.

"I do," Floyd said. "I've got a big fight coming up over the weekend. I can't afford to miss even a day of workouts."

"We all miss you," Mardee said. "Do you ever think about going back to the ranch?"

Floyd shook his head negatively. "Not right now," he said decisively. "I've got things to do and places to see." He smiled down at his sister. Then he bent down swiftly and gave her a kiss on the forehead. "Take care of that boy,"

That boy, Mardee thought ruefully. That boy that has the same blue eyes as you. She had noticed the similar color of their eyes as well as the fond tender look in Floyd's face when he held the baby. I think I've discovered the reason Lola wanted to make sure her baby had the Spencer name. I doubt there was ever a relationship with the sawmill worker she told me about.

Addie had food prepared at her house for the funeral dinner. Mardee ate little, but she appreciated the kind words and thoughts of the people who were there supporting her. Finally, when the crowd started to clear out, Mardee went and sat in the swing on the porch. As she pushed it listlessly back and forth, she realized she felt nothing but emptiness. I'll never love again, she told herself. I'll never really live again. She laid her head back and closed her eyes. There were no tears now. I've cried enough tears to last me a lifetime, she thought sadly.

Suddenly she felt the weight of someone sitting down beside her. She opened her eyes and saw her companion was Jeff. She sat up straight and looked him straight in the face. "Thank you so much for everything you've done, Jeff," she said. "You helped Papa and me so much in making the arrangements. You took some of the agony out of it all for me. I appreciate you more than I can say."

"You know I'd do anything for you, Mardee. I've been proud to be allowed to help you."

There was more silence as Mardee's mind traveled back several years to the last time she and Jeff sat in this swing together. He had told her he was marrying another woman. But he had also told her to never doubt the love he had felt for her. Confusing, Mardee thought. Too complicated for me to figure out today. Then her thoughts came back to the present and ideas for the future started stirring. Finally, she said, "I'm not sure what I'm going to do, Jeff. But I may want to leave Santa Fe. It would be hard to stay here without Carter."

"I can understand that," Jeff said. "I'll help you do whatever you have to do."

A sudden idea started forming in Mardee's head. "Would you be interested in buying out my part of the law firm?"

"Perhaps," Jeff said after a pause. "We'll all have to think about it, and, of course, we'll have to consult Will. He and I do get along well, though. I doubt he'd have any objections."

"What I've been thinking about, Jeff, is going back to the Manzanos. Papa and Mother Spencer are getting old. Papa has incurred some indebtedness. His business isn't apparently doing as well as usual. I could sell my home and the business, and I'd have the money to help them pay off their note at the bank. Roy is the only one at the ranch to help them now, and they could use me. What do you think of that idea?"

"There's merit to it," Jeff said slowly.

"And I could raise Robbie Blue there," Mardee said, excitement mounting in her voice.

"That would be a good place to raise a boy," Jeff agreed. "He'd grow strong and sturdy, running over those hills. You'd have to let me send Beth up there in the summertime."

"Oh yes, "Mardee said enthusiastically. "And I'll teach them to ride."

"Of course," Jeff said with a grin. "And they'll try to outrun everybody who rides a horse to the place."

Mardee smiled as she thought of her challenge to beat Jeff in a horse race so many years ago. Then she said seriously, "It just seems like a good place to go now. A place to heal, maybe."

"And a place to grow," Jeff said gently. "The first woman lawyer in New Mexico could set up her office in Mountainair when she feels strong enough. And that would be a stepping stone to entering politics someday. Women will have the vote soon, thanks in part to your hard work, and you would get all the female votes. You should make a successful politician."

"Not so fast," Mardee said, but the gleam was back in her eyes. "First, let's get you elected to the Attorney General's office."

"Actually, I've been asked to run," Jeff said. "After Christmas I'm going to make a definite decision on entering that race."

"Well," Mardee said, "That sounds like a good plan to me. I'll help you."

Jeff rose and looked down into Mardee's upturned face. "I've got to go and pick up Beth," he said apologetically. "Are you going to be all right?"

"I'm going to be fine," Mardee said resolutely. "The last time I saw Carter he assured me I could climb every mountain, and I naively told him I could do that because I had all the hardest ones climbed. Little did I know what was going to happen to me in the near future, but I really do have the hardest ones climbed now, and I will climb the rest of them easily, you bet! Robbie Blue and I will climb them together."

Jeff gazed in awe at the radiant upturned face of the woman he had loved so long. "My dear," he said gently, "you've done well in Santa Fe. Your imprint is on the education system because of your work in the governor's office. Every child in our state has equal rights to an education, and you've also worked hard for voting rights for women in New Mexico."

Jeff took Mardee's hands and held them tightly as he continued to gaze at this amazing woman whom he had loved since he had met her in the Manzano Mountains so long ago. He saw the winter sun catch the gold in her hair and turn it to fire. "I'm betting on you," he said. "I'm betting on this outstanding Santa Fe woman."

He put his arms around her and drew her close. She leaned into his embrace, but her eyes were focused over his shoulder as she gazed toward the west. Her heart was traveling ahead of her body, and she was already visualizing a new beginning in her beloved Manzano Mountains.